The Road
to Hope

Crissi Langwell

Hope Series
Book 1

Copyright © 2014 Crissi Langwell and
North Coast Stories

Photos by Kent Sorensen at kentwsorensen.com,
and Samot/Shutterstock, Inc.
Cover design by Liz Carrasco

ISBN-10: 0989066088
ISBN-13: 978-0-9890660-8-2

This book is also available as an e-book. Please visit the author's website to find out where it can be purchased.

www.crissilangwell.com

To my husband, Shawn, who is my rock.

Table of Contents

Jill Johnson

- One -
The Point of Impact

There was no stopping it. In one moment, Toby had been standing in the front of the small shopping cart, grinning at his mom as she filled a bag with green beans. In the next, the cart tipped forward against his weight, sending him head-first toward the checkered linoleum in the middle of Hal's Market. The look of terror on her toddler's face was etched in Jill's mind as she saw him tumble from the cart, falling just far enough away that she knew she'd never reach him in time. But in the eternity that lay in those few seconds, she made a valiant effort, throwing her arms forward to catch nothing but air.

Toby's forehead hit the slick floor first, the rest of his body crumpling down into his neck, then careening over his body like a rag doll. Jill reached him and, despite everything she had ever learned about not moving accident victims, she turned him over to see if he was okay. She would never forget the look in his eyes. Tearless, they reached into her, grabbing at her guilt with a firm hold while raking over her worst fears. Then they lost all recognition.

"Toby," she breathed. His olive eyes were fixed on the ceiling, the blank expression frozen on his face. But then his body relaxed into a deep and shuddering breath, followed by a scream of pain and terror. His cries were a sweet sound to Jill's ears. She scooped her son up and held him tight against her chest.

Jill avoided the stares from the small crowd forming around her and Toby. She could feel the weight of their judgment, their unspoken thoughts screaming at her. *How could she? What kind of mother lets that happen? She doesn't deserve a child.* Jill held her sobbing son to her chest, rocking him next to the green beans and zucchini while trying to pretend the growing crowd didn't exist. The two of them sat until his screams subsided into hiccupped breathing. Then Toby lay his curly blonde head against her shoulder, playing with a lock of her chestnut hair as he breathed into her sweater. Jill couldn't help but see the irony in this—her injured toddler finding safety in the very person who had let him fall.

Once home, Jill carried Toby into the house and placed him in his playpen. She studied him for a moment, taking in his dimpled grin underneath the purple goose egg forming on his forehead. She reached forward to touch it with her finger, but he grabbed her hand and laughed.

"You silly thing," Jill chuckled, shaking her finger in his little hand and soaking up his giggles. "Mommy will be right back. I just have to get the grocery bags." She left him to play in his playpen while she gathered the groceries from her car. But when she returned, she found her husband kneeling beside the mesh enclosure where Toby sat playing, gently brushing his son's hair aside to get a better look at his forehead.

Michael looked up at her, and Jill flashed him a quick smile. But it faded as she saw the look of concern flash across his eyes. He looked back at Toby, lifting the curls from his forehead again.

"How did this happen?" he asked, delicately tracing the purple mark on their son's head. If it hurt, Toby didn't seem to notice. He was busy studying the blocks he was knocking around in the playpen, clanking them together with a concentrated look on his face—as if playing were his job.

Jill studied the look on her husband's face, trying to gauge what he was thinking. Was his tone accusatory? Did he already blame her, even before knowing the circumstances? She tensed up, ready to defend herself against any accusations that might come her way. But she could see nothing incriminating in his eyes.

"He was standing at the edge of the cart and it just tipped," she told him. She waited for him to come unglued, to demand to know how any mother could be so careless with her child. But he only inspected the bump for a moment longer, then turned away from the playpen and stood up.

"Must have been scary," was all he said, offering her a kind smile and touching her on the arm. Jill breathed a sigh of relief.

"It was terrifying," she admitted. "One moment he was fine, and then he was flying through the air. The look on his face…" She trailed off, shuddering as she thought of how vacant his eyes had been before he came back to her, regaining his senses. "And the people! They all stopped to stare at us. I've never felt so judged in my life! None of them offered to help or to even see if he was okay."

"*Is* he okay? Do you think we should call a doctor?" Michael asked. They both looked at their son as he quietly played in the playpen.

"I think he's all right, now," Jill said. "He's fallen plenty of times, though never this hard…" She let the last words trail off as she tried to convince herself again that she wasn't some horrible mother.

"You're probably right," Michael agreed. "Still, let's just keep a close eye on him. If anything seems odd, we'll take him in." He followed Jill into the kitchen where the two of them unpacked the groceries from the bags. "What's for dinner?" he asked her. She looked up at the weekly meal list they kept on the refrigerator door.

"Looks like it's your turn to cook," she said, tracing her finger to where Thursday night's meal was on the list. "Yup, it's all you. And you're making Chicken Piccata," she said with a grin. The dish was a specialty he had first wowed her with in the early days of their courtship, and still one of her favorites.

"Dang," he said, wrinkling his nose at the prospect of cooking. "Did you buy any more capers? I believe you ate the last of them with breakfast this morning." Jill ducked her head with a sheepish grin. The tiny pickled pearls were her latest food obsession, adding them to almost every meal she ate. Because of this, she made sure she'd picked up several more jars at the store, tossing one of them over to Michael before placing the rest in the cabinet. "Chicken Piccata it is, m'lady," he said with an exaggerated curtsy. "Think you can toss a salad for me?"

Jill put the last of the groceries away while Michael prepared dinner, then grabbed the ingredients for the salad. She chopped up the lettuce, throwing it in a bowl with cranberries, feta cheese and pecans. In the hallway, Toby was softly singing to himself as he played in his playpen. Jill glanced over at her son from where she stood in the kitchen, smiling as she watched him play with one of his trucks. He was lying next to it, rolling it near his head while his sleepy eyes fought to stay open. He looked in her direction when he realized he had an audience. Pushing the truck aside, he scrambled to his feet and hung over the edge of the playpen.

"Up!" he called to her, holding his arms out to her, his face crumpling as he prepared to cry.

"Oh, you're not really upset," Jill cooed as she came over and swooped him up. He broke into a grin, his complaints forgotten as he bounced in her arms. His head hit Jill's chin, the pain coursing through Jill like an electric shock. They both froze, and she fought the urge to cry out. She took a deep breath in and out, grinning at Toby, hoping to avoid a toddler meltdown if he was hurt, too. To her relief, he mimicked her smile.

"Ooh!" she cooed at him. "You're Mommy's strong boy, aren't you?" she asked him. He wriggled in her arms, laughing as Jill gritted her teeth against her throbbing chin. She made sure to turn her head to the side to prevent being hit again as he bounced against her. "Are you hungry?" she asked him, and he nodded with wide eyes.

"Humbree!" he said, and then laughed as his mom pretended to eat his belly. Jill while airplaned him to the kitchen and then landed him in his highchair. Michael had already prepared a small bowl of cut-up chicken and broccoli, and Jill raced to place a bib on him before he grabbed at the bowl. Toby slammed his hand into the food while holding a fork in his other hand.

"Use your fork, sweetheart," Jill coaxed. Toby waved his fork in the air as if to show her where it was, then continued to feed himself with his food-filled fist. "Guess we'll work on that," she sighed with a smile to Michael. She sat down and he set a plate in front of her. Closing her eyes, she took a deep breath in, smiling at the meal's aroma. "Thank you, honey," she said as he took the seat next to her.

Michael told her about his day at the office, rehashing a conversation he'd held with a client. Jill smiled and nodded, trying to listen. But her mind kept revisiting the afternoon at the grocery store. While Toby was fine, she still felt terrible that he'd even fallen from the cart in the first place. When she had described the accident to Michael, Jill had purposely left out the conversation with the manager of the store following the fall. But it was that conversation that haunted her. The short, shrew woman had pulled her aside once Toby had recovered, barely giving her son a sideways glance as he sniffled into his mother's sweater.

"You know, there are signs on the cart to prevent accidents like this from happening," the woman had told her, pointing to a similar sign that was on the wall near where they stood. Her accusatory tone paralyzed Jill in her defenses, leaving her only able to nod and apologize for breaking the rules. Jill knew the manager was only protecting her store from being sued as the woman went on about safety issues. Still her face burned hot with shame as the woman continued, making it clear that any lawsuits Jill brought upon the store might have Child Protective Services knocking on her door.

"Perhaps you would do best if you took parenting seriously," the woman had chastised her, making the final blow on the wedge that was pounding into Jill's conscience.

"Well, besides Toby becoming an acrobat in the store, anything exciting happen today?" Michael asked her. Jill shook herself out of her thoughts and back to the table.

"Not really," she said. "I met with Lucy earlier today so that the kids could play while we caught up." Lucy was Jill's best friend, a title she had claimed since the two were in grade school. Back then they had gossiped about boys and the latest Hollywood heartthrob in the confines of Lucy's pink bedroom. Now, it was mostly about Lucy's two girls and Toby, allowing motherhood to become the new backbone of their friendship.

"It's been awhile since you two saw each other, hasn't it? How is she?" Michael asked.

"She's good. Well, sort of. Phil's been working longer hours at the office, and she's a little frazzled about being left so long with the kids. She's starting to feel like a single mother. But I think it's getting easier now that the girls are older. Did you realize Cassie starts kindergarten in the fall?"

"That's crazy!" Michael exclaimed. "Wasn't she just a baby last year?"

"Seriously! I can't believe how fast they grow." Jill looked at Toby as he pushed the food around on his tray. His soft curls framed his face, offering hints of the infant he once was while revealing glimpses of the boy he'd soon be in several years' time. "Just think, before we know it he'll be asking for the car keys," she joked. As if on cue, Toby rubbed his eyes, his face twisting into a cranky scowl. He pushed his bowl off his high chair and it landed with a clang, scattering remnants of his dinner all over the floor.

"I think someone's ready for bed," Jill mused. "What's your choice, cleanup or getting the baby to go to sleep?" She stood in front of him with her hands poised in a mock roshambo posture, grimacing as Toby amped up his complaints when he wasn't picked up right away. Michael took one look at the piles of dishes in the kitchen and pointed at the baby. While a wonderful cook, he had yet to learn the fine art of using less pots and pans, or even just cleaning as he went along.

"Toby enjoys my reading better, anyway," Michael said, scooting just out of reach when Jill swatted at him.

"Typical," she said, wrinkling her nose with a grin. She removed the tray from the highchair so that Michael could reach their screaming son. Toby immediately stopped crying as soon as Michael picked him up, his little face transforming from a painful grimace to a shining smile. "Look at those crocodile tears," Jill cooed into her son's beaming face. "What an actor you are!" She leaned in to give Toby a kiss before Michael took him down the hall to start his bath. And then she set about cleaning the kitchen. As she cleared the plates from the table she could hear her husband giving voices to the various ships that sailed the murky seas of Toby's bathwater, the torrential storms prevailing as soapy water splashed all over the bathroom. Shaking her head with amusement, she settled into the dishes, filling the sink with water and adding a touch of soap until the chaos in front of her became a mass of soothing white foam. Jill plunged her hands into the warm water, allowing the action of washing one dish at a time to pull her away from the messy kitchen, the shopping carts, the judging eyes and the store manager who told her she was a bad parent. In her meditation, she focused instead on the calm sensation washing over her, pushing out the feelings of guilt that had become her primary emotion that day.

So he fell. He survived, right? Life is full of bumps and bruises, and sometimes the biggest ones are from those we love and trust. I am not a bad mother. I am not a bad mother. I am not a bad mother.

Jill closed her eyes and inhaled deeply, repeating those words over and over in a whisper until they felt like a foreign language on her lips.

"You're not a bad mother," Michael said from behind her, wrapping his arms around her from behind and brushing his lips against her neck. Jill opened her eyes and smiled sheepishly. She was tempted to tell him about the store manager, how she seemed to think otherwise.

"I'm just, well...you know," she stammered, deciding mid-sentence that she couldn't bring herself to talk about it. Michael kissed her cheek, and she turned to the side so he could reach her mouth. With her hands still submerged in the soapy water, he teased her lips with the tip of his tongue in a sensual suggestion that the dishes needed to wait. After four years of marriage, she still got butterflies from the taste of his kiss. She didn't need to explain anything. He already knew, just as he knew everything about her. "I have to finish the dishes," she whispered against his lips, and he smiled back against her mouth with a low hum.

"Would you like any help?" he asked, though she could tell in his eyes that he was hoping she would say no.

"Go relax," she told him. "I only have ten more minutes of work here. I'll watch TV with you in a few before we go to bed." She pecked him on the cheek before he left, and then set about finishing the final dishes and wiping down the counters until there was no trace of the night's dinner. After taking out the trash, she collapsed with an exaggerated sigh of relief on the couch, enticing a chuckle from Michael before they both settled into the shows flashing across the TV screen.

It was their usual routine, a night in on the couch. *How drastically life changes after having kids*, Jill mused, even as she enjoyed their usual pace. She looked at her husband on the couch, smiling at the salt and pepper hint of a beard on his face. She ran her hand against his cheek, and he leaned into it so she could get the full effect of his coarse stubble against her soft hand. He looked at her sideways with one eye closed, the dimple at the corner of his mouth making him even more irresistible.

"Have I ever told you that I love you?" she asked him. He squinted, looking up at the ceiling as if trying to remember.

"Nope, I don't think you have," he teased her. He ducked as she swatted at him with a throw pillow from the couch.

"Well I do, you big jerk. Sometimes you're even kind of cute."

"Really? Tell me more," he said, grabbing the pillow from her and tucking it under his arm to keep it away from her.

"I also think you're pretty full of yourself," she said.

"Well, when you're this good-looking…" he said, stroking his chin and giving her a wink. She giggled as he grabbed at her, finally catching her and then holding her against the couch. She didn't give much of a fight, grinning up at him. "I think you're pretty cute yourself, young lady," he told her, and then growled while he burrowed his scratchy face into her neck. She shivered, grinning at the sensation of both being tickled and having chills run all over her body in one movement.

"Wait! I thought we were watching TV!" she laughed. He took the remote and turned the television off.

"Nothing's on," he grinned, and then busied himself in unbuttoning her shirt before slipping it off. The rest of her clothes followed suit, and the two of them hid underneath the blanket from the back of the couch, giggling in a flurry of kisses and caresses. The outside world was forgotten as they searched for anything left unexplored on each other's body. And when the last mystery was uncovered, they wrapped their arms around each other and fell asleep under the blanket. It was nearly three in the morning before they stirred enough to get up, gather their clothes from the floor, and move to sleep in their bed until the sun woke up.

- Two -
The End of Innocence

Jill kept her eyes closed when Michael kissed her on the cheek in the morning.

"Babe," he whispered. "I'm leaving for work." Her eyelids felt weighted down as she opened them. He was standing next to her, his face obscured by the bright sunlight streaming in the window behind him.

"Mmmph," she grunted, rolling over. "What time is it?"

"It's still early," he said. "But you're on toddler duty now."

"Where's Toby?"

"I didn't have time to check on him, but I think he's still sleeping. At least, he hasn't started crying yet. Go ahead and sleep a little more, the baby monitor is on your nightstand."

Jill smiled. "Thank you," she murmured. "Have a good day."

"You too, sweetheart. Get some rest. I love you."

"I love you, too," she said, then burrowed her way under the covers to catch a few more minutes of sleep.

It was nearly an hour later when she found her way out from under her pillow to look at the clock. 8:30, and the baby monitor was still silent. "Thank goodness," she sighed. He had slept in.

Jill pulled back the covers and swung her feet over the bed and into her slippers. Slipping her robe over her shoulders, she walked down the hall. Toby's door was slightly ajar, and she peeked through the crack. His back was to her in the crib as he slept, and she refrained from opening the door any further to avoid waking him up.

In the kitchen, the light was glowing red on the coffee pot. She poured herself a cup, and inhaled the steam that wet her face when she brought the coffee to her lips. Ignoring the slightly burnt taste from being left on the burner too long, Jill focused on waking up. She smiled and closed her eyes as a moment from the night before flashed through her mind like an electric spark. Four years of marriage, and she and Michael still felt passion for each other. Another jolt went through her as she remembered the intensity in his eyes when he looked at her, and then the excitement she felt when he lowered his gaze to attend to her needs.

Jill shook her head, chuckling. Here she was, reliving a smoldering moment while wearing her ratty bathrobe and holding a burnt cup of coffee in her hand. At this rate, it would be noon before she got Toby up and dressed.

"Toby!" she sang out, wondering just how long her toddler was going to stay asleep. She padded back toward Toby's room with her coffee in hand, ready to rouse her sleepy boy.

Something wasn't right. She could feel it in the pit of her stomach as soon as she pushed the door open. Toby was still lying in his crib. A sour odor overwhelmed the room. There was no sound in the room, as if the air had been sucked right out. Toby wasn't moving. Not even a little. Jill crept closer, her breath moving in and out in shallow gusts as her heart beat against her throat. She peered over at her baby boy, freezing at the sight of his grey skin, his open mouth, the small stain of vomit that had soaked into the sheet beneath him. His eyes remained shut, but he no longer appeared to be sleeping. His body was still. Too still. There was no rise or fall in his chest, no pursing of his lips, no perspiration in his blonde curls against his forehead.

Jill reached out to touch him, but stopped just short of reaching his cheek. She couldn't. If her hand felt the coolness of his skin, it would be real. Instead, she stared at his chest, willing it to move up and down.

Wake up, Toby. Wake up. Just open your eyes. Come on, I'll take you to the doctor. All you have to do is wake up.

He never moved. And it was only moments later when Jill realized she'd dropped her coffee on the tan carpet of his room, the dark brown stain spreading beneath his crib as she vomited into his toy box.

When there was nothing left in her, she remained on the floor, kneeling next to Toby's crib. She stayed close to the floor so she couldn't see his face. But his tiny fist lay near the slats of his crib, curled up against the soft fabric of his mattress sheet. With shaking hands, she moved her hand close to his, resting her fingers on the material beside him. She inched her finger closer until she finally reached his tiny fingernail. The coolness in his skin was unmistakable as she moved his finger, trying to coax the life back into him. Nothing. She wrapped her finger around his hand, gasping at the icy feel.

He was gone.

Her thoughts raced, but nothing seemed to make sense. It was as if a giant block was placed in the middle of her brain. She didn't know what to do next. Who did she call first? How was she going to tell Michael? What would she say?

She picked up the phone, and her fingers took over for her.

"9-1-1, state your emergency," a monotone voice said over the line.

"I—I—I…" she started, the words stuck in her throat.

"Ma'am, is everything okay? Your emergency?" the woman said, softening at her panic.

"I think… I think my baby is dead." A sob escaped her throat as soon as the words poured out, followed by a shriek, a sound so strange it didn't feel like it belonged to her. She could hear herself screaming, feel the hysteria within her chest. But it all felt like a lie.

He's not dead. He can't be. We were just playing yesterday. We have so much more to do today. He has a whole life to grow into tomorrow, and the next day, and the day after that.

He's not dead. He can't be.

"Ma'am, I need you to stay calm. Help is on the way," the woman urged her over the line. Jill managed to rein in her screams, feeling them fighting against her throat as she held her hand over her mouth. The operator asked her several more questions, and Jill could hear the sirens coming closer. It was all becoming more real. And Michael still didn't know. It was a phone call she didn't want to make. She didn't want to hurt him. Whatever words she gave him, it would take being a daddy away from him. She was scared of what that would do to him. And she was scared that every time he looked at her, it would be with blame in his eyes. He might never be able to look at her with love again.

She could hear the paramedics knocking on the front door, and she managed to let the operator on the phone know before hanging up. Two men in blue uniforms rushed into the room, one of them coming to her side to help her stand, peppering her with questions as the other checked on Toby.

"Please, I need to call my husband," she whispered. The questions stopped. The other paramedic slowed his movements as it became clear that no help could bring Toby back.

"Of course," the man closest to her said. He rested his hand on her arm as the other paramedic lowered the side of Toby's crib so he could move her son's tiny body to the gurney. Jill fought back a sob as he lifted Toby up, his little arms dangling beneath him. "We'll give you a ride to the hospital. You can call from the ambulance."

The man held on to Jill's arm as they walked behind the gurney. She didn't even bother locking the door, and only grabbed her purse as a second thought. She was thankful for the guide to the ambulance, feeling the weight of her neighbors' eyes following her every move, reminiscent of the weight of stares she'd felt the day before in the grocery store.

I'm not fit to be a mother. I couldn't even keep him safe. I deserved to lose him.

"Petaluma Press," the receptionist said over the phone. Jill hadn't even known she'd dialed the number.

"Michael, please," she whispered into her cellphone.

"Excuse me? Is someone there?"

"Michael Johnson," she said louder. "I need to speak to my husband, Michael. It's urgent."

The paramedic that had walked her to the ambulance was sitting in the back of the vehicle with her, staying near Toby's covered body. He didn't look at her, but stayed fixated on the sheet that covered her son. Jill couldn't help wondering if this was just a normal part of his job, transporting dead children and grieving mothers to the hospital.

"Hi honey, what's up?" Michael asked on the other end of the line. Her heart pounded at his voice, the words she needed to say tasting rotten in her mouth.

"Mike, something happened," she said.

"What's wrong?" he asked. "Are you okay? Is Toby okay?" She could hear his breath in the phone, the panic framing his words like the fear that was frozen inside her.

"No," she said. She whimpered, unable to say the words. The paramedic looked up at her, compassion in his eyes. She stifled her sobs, taking a deep breath. "Please," she told Michael. "You need to meet me at the hospital."

"What's going on, Jill," Michael demanded. Was he angry, or just scared? Jill couldn't tell. She could imagine him standing, attracting attention from his coworkers.

"Toby…" she began, but couldn't finish. She didn't need to. His sob in the phone told her it was enough.

"I'm on my way," he managed to get out in a shaky voice before the line went dead.

A few hours later, Jill sat next to Michael in a small office at the hospital. The doctor sat in front of them, wearing a white lab coat buttoned against his chest and a compassionate look on his kind face. Jill kept forgetting his name, even though he had told them only minutes earlier. She kept glancing at the patch on his jacket to remind herself. *Dr. Weiler.* She looked around the office, focusing on the many framed certificates he had covering the walls. She looked at them, but she couldn't see any of them. It was like the words were all in gibberish. Nothing seemed real. Her hands felt like lead against her thighs as she sat in the hard chair on the other side of the doctor's desk. She lifted her hands just to see if they were still hers, then let them drop against her legs. They seemed foreign. Everything did.

Michael took her hand in his, squeezing it tight before loosening his grasp again. He proceeded to move his finger against her skin, caressing her in an attempt to calm her. It felt forced. But Jill didn't stop him, relaxing into his touch and letting her husband absorb the fidgetiness inside her.

"We won't know anything for certain until the autopsy," Dr. Weiler said. "But by appearances, it looks like he had a concussion."

"The fall," Jill breathed, and Michael tightened his grasp on her. The doctor looked up and gave her a gentle nod. Earlier she had been asked about every mark on his body, including the dark lump on his forehead. A man in a business suit had come in later to ask more about the injury. Her hands had trembled as she described the event. If she hadn't felt so numb, she may have even broke down crying. But instead, she looked at her hands in her lap as she gave him every detail she could recall. How she had let Toby stand in the shopping cart. How it couldn't hold his weight. How he fell against the linoleum. How he had looked at her. How everyone had looked at her. How she had failed as a mother.

Michael had kept his arm around her the whole time as she answered more questions about life at home, what kind of child Toby was, and what had happened earlier in the day before the fall. She had let the answers roll off her tongue involuntarily. She was ready for it all to be over. She hadn't even cared if he decided to lock her up for being a bad mother. Nothing mattered anymore.

But he hadn't locked her up. He just offered his condolences and thanked her for her time before leaving.

"Yes, the fall," the doctor echoed. "From the CAT scan, it appears Toby hit his head hard enough to shake his brain. This caused some minor swelling. However, it may not have been the concussion that killed him." The doctor paused, shuffling through the papers on his desk before setting them in a neat stack beside him. He removed his glasses and cleared his throat before looking at the couple before him.

Jill held her breath, unsure if she could handle anymore.

"When the brain goes through trauma like Toby's did, it can cause a wave of seasickness. It appears Toby vomited in his sleep, and he may have choked on it."

The room became smaller, the air more stale. Jill felt her body go numb as the words pounded into her head.

"So if we had taken Toby to the hospital earlier, he'd be alive right now, wouldn't he?" Michael asked. A pained look flashed across the doctor's face before he composed himself.

"We can't be sure," the doctor said, averting his eyes. Jill could tell he was just being diplomatic. If she had listened to Michael's concerns and let a doctor take a look at him, Toby wouldn't be dead. Her body shook, her tears no longer able to stay back. She took her hand from Michael's grasp to cover her face. He lifted his arm and wrapped it around her shoulder, and she couldn't help but wonder why. She had killed their son. She could feel the silent way he cried, only making her cry more.

"Thank you for your time," Michael managed to choke out. "I think we need to go home now."

- Three -
The Space Between Seconds

The trees outside were in full bloom now. Spring had made way for summer, which had always been Jill's favorite season. But she hardly noticed it this year. For almost three months, she had only been able to drag herself from the bed to the couch, laying there to stare out the window, but seeing nothing. The house felt dark inside, even with every curtain open to let the light in. She longed to feel the sun on her. But today, just like every morning in Northern California, was cloudy and overcast. Even when the sun was shining she couldn't see it. The whole house was closing in on her and she was suffocating.

She didn't think she'd ever get used to the overwhelming silence of a home without Toby.

Down the hall, the door to Toby's room remained closed. The night they came home from the hospital, Michael took it upon himself to clean the room of the soiled toys in the toy box and the sheet on Toby's bed. Then he closed the door, and it remained that way ever since. It nearly killed Jill every time she walked by. Sometimes she could almost hear Toby laughing inside, or even calling to her to come get him. But she was afraid she'd lose her mind if she ever opened the door to peek inside; she was afraid to see the emptiness of a room that used to hold so much life.

In the beginning, friends had tried to come over and see what they could do to help. Lucy would come over with her young girls, her neighbors would bring casserole dishes and flowers, and even a few acquaintances from the toddler playgroup would stop by to see how she was doing. Jill was polite with them, but the visits were overwhelming. While her friends' intentions were good, it only twisted the knife of reality that her son was gone. It was especially hard to hear the laughter of children who weren't hers echoing off the hardwood floors and vacant walls. With a heavy heart, she began to turn people away at the door, telling them she just needed space. After a while, they just stopped coming over altogether.

Toby's absence was also taking a toll on her marriage. Michael left for work every morning, and she could see the relief in his eyes when it was time to go. As much as she knew he was grieving, she knew she was the one bringing him down further. She felt like a disease, like the weighted cloud that was cast upon her might spread to anyone who came in contact with her. Michael had once brought up the topic of counseling, hinting at the dark shadow that had become her life. But she couldn't. To relive that awful morning over and over with a stranger…. It couldn't happen.

But she knew that the shadow of depression was enveloping her slowly, consuming her until she was just a whisper of a person. She no longer felt close to Michael. She couldn't even remember the last time he had touched her. In the days after Toby's death, it had come so naturally. They had bonded together in grief, turning to each other to find solace within the shock of their new reality. Michael had taken some time off of work and stayed home with Jill. At night they would hold each other under the heavy blankets. But intimacy became something different. It no longer felt appropriate. The few times they tried to make love, the grief was always there, quenching any passion that dared to flare up. So they resorted to holding each other for a little while, then moving to their own separate sides of the bed before sleep took over. Eventually even that brief connection time was lost to their sadness, and they'd adjourn to bed without even touching each other at all.

The most unbearable part was the deafening silence that took over the house. With Michael at work, the only sound was the tick of the second hand from the clock in the kitchen. Jill hadn't even noticed it before. But without anyone to move around her, the clock pounded into her head. Tick. Tick. Tick. TICK. She was tempted to take the batteries out and go through the day in a timeless manner. But the thought of losing the noise unnerved her even more than just hearing it all day long. She wasn't sure if the absence of the second hand click would make the house utterly silent, or reveal a new noise that would drive her closer to insanity. So she let the second hand continue its path around the numbered face, counting down every second further away from when she was once called Mama.

Next to the couch, Jill could see the face of her cellphone light up with a call. Michael's name and smiling face appeared on the phone, a photo that was taken before they knew the extent of mortality—that death could even claim the lives of children. She considered letting it go to voicemail; the thought of speaking at all pained her at times. But before the final ring, she grabbed it and answered.

"How are you?" Michael asked. She wasn't sure if he was asking out of obligation, or if he truly was concerned.

"I'm okay," she told him. She forgot what feeling okay was like. But if it meant how she felt like every other day, than she felt okay.

"Have you eaten anything yet today?" he asked.

"I had some toast," she lied.

"I made you a sandwich and left it in the fridge," he told her. "Try to eat some of it today, okay?"

Despite herself, she smiled at the gesture.

"Thank you," she told him.

"Do you think you might be able to get out of the house?" he asked her. "Perhaps get some fresh air?"

"Perhaps," she said.

"Well, I need to stay late at work today, and I don't have time to stop at the grocery store…" Michael trailed off, but Jill could hear the question in his voice.

"You need me to do the shopping, don't you?" she guessed.

"Yeah. I mean, if it's not too much trouble, that is."

Jill hadn't left the house since Toby died. Well, once. But that was the funeral, and she couldn't even remember any of it for it to count. Their parents had banded together to coordinate the details, and all she and Michael had to do was show up, say thank you to anyone who offered them condolences, and then leave when everyone was done eating from the deli trays in the banquet room of the church. Other than that, she stayed indoors and away from people. She was certain that anyone who saw her would see "mother of dead baby" printed all over her body.

"I don't know…" she began, tears springing into her eyes. She knew she should. Michael had been carrying the full weight of the house since Toby died. She felt guilty about this, knowing she needed to somehow break free from the darkness that enveloped her so she could ease his burden. After all, her husband deserved to grieve, too. But she couldn't, or rather, she didn't know how. Besides, if she did get up and begin living life again, what did that say about how much she loved her son? If she could go on without him, did that make her less of a mother to him?

"It's okay," Michael said quickly. "I'll just tell my boss I can't stay late, and just leave earlier tomorrow to get the rest of this project done."

"No," Jill said. She forced herself to sit up, aware of the weight in her head as she did. "I should do it. I mean, I can do it."

"Are you sure? I don't want to push you. But it might be good for you to get dressed and get out of the house."

"I guess so," she said.

"Thank you sweetheart. I left a list on the kitchen table in case you could," he told her. Jill jerked her head in surprise, resentment sparking inside her at his assumptions. He had planned this. It wasn't some surprise.

"You knew you needed me to shop today?" she asked.

"Actually, I leave a list on the table every Wednesday. You just never notice it," he told her. Jill's resentment simmered, her guilt bubbling up once more. "Please eat lunch first, though," he reminded her, as if she were a child. It made her realize just how much he had assumed the caretaker role since Toby died.

"I will," she promised before they said their goodbyes and hung up.

Jill stared out the window for a moment, trying to remember what she needed to do first. *Brush my teeth. No, eat first.* She got up from the couch, her legs like lead as she placed one step in front of the other. The list of food lay on the table, and she picked it up before she grabbed the sandwich out of the refrigerator that Michael had made for her. Each bite was like clay in her mouth, but she continued to eat it, noticing how the emptiness inside was slowly disappearing. The usual items were listed one by one on the slip of paper. Bread, milk, eggs. She couldn't help but notice how small the list was before realizing *why*. There were no diapers, no Cheerios, no jars of baby food… Jill closed her eyes and took a deep breath in and held it for a moment, wishing the rest of her world would stop breathing as well. Only when her chest ached did she let it out again.

She only finished half of her sandwich, hiding the rest of it under some paper towels in the garbage in case Michael was checking. Then she went to their bedroom and undressed. She avoided her emaciated image in the mirror, sidestepping the scale so she wouldn't know how much weight she'd lost, and slipped under the running water in the shower. She stood without moving for a full ten minutes, letting the water pelt her skin before she even touched the soap and shampoo. Then she put her sweatpants and sweater back on after drying, hoping they were at least clean enough to be seen in public. She remembered to brush her teeth, then grabbed her purse to leave.

It felt strange to be behind the wheel of her car again. It wasn't like learning to drive, but it did feel like something she hadn't done in many years. Jill navigated the streets of Petaluma, taking the roads through town to avoid the freeway. She purposefully passed by Hal's Market, unable to look in its direction. She knew they wouldn't remember her. They wouldn't even wonder where Toby was, or ask about his fall. But if Jill had to walk in and see the exact square on the linoleum where his head had hit, she might forget how to breathe. So instead, Jill drove to Food Mart, the outlet grocery store on the other side of town.

The parking lot was already full by the time she got there, despite the fact that it was just after noon and most people were at work. Jill maneuvered her car to the furthest corner of the lot where she found a tight space between two older cars. It was a few stalls down from where a crowd had formed around a taco truck, mostly made up of workers from the vineyards that surrounded Petaluma. Judging by their soiled clothing and faces hidden under hats, it appeared they had just come in from the fields. A few of them looked Jill's way, offering a quick nod when their eyes met before averting their gaze. Most of them, however, paid her no attention at all.

Jill followed behind a mom leading a chain of children holding hands behind her. Hers wasn't the only family like that; there were many more trains of children making their way from the parking lot, funneling into the sliding doors of the store. Some of the kids had food stains on their clothes, with hair that flew in all directions as if brushing had gone out of style. Looking at the coffee drops on the front of her own sweater, Jill realized she had no room to judge. But she did marvel at how willingly they accepted their job just to hold the hand of their sibling in front of them, allowing themselves to be led into the store without getting lost.

The front of the store was a bottleneck as each family waited to get their cart. Jill stood behind a large woman, trying not to look at the toddler she held in her arms. Finally, she made it to the front. She went to grab her cart, but found it locked to the ones behind them. She shook it, trying to break it free. It wouldn't budge.

"You need a quarter," a woman said behind her. Jill turned her head, and the blonde woman, probably about twenty years old, snapped her gum impatiently. Behind her was a fidgeting line of people, all peering around the woman to see what the holdup was. "A quarter," the woman repeated, holding her own coin up. Looking through the line once more, Jill realized she was the only one not holding a quarter.

"Oh," Jill said, feeling stupid. She looked at the cart, and saw the coin slot near the handle. "I didn't know." She pulled her wallet out of her purse and unzipped the part holding her change. Then she fished around through the pennies, hoping by some miracle a quarter would appear.

"Here," the woman said, and she pushed her quarter into the slot. "I've been there." Jill realized that maybe her hasty dressing job was giving off the wrong impression.

"Are you sure?" she asked the girl, who only smiled back.

"I have more," the girl reassured her. Jill thanked her and then pulled the cart back. With the quarter in place, the cart glided toward her without effort. Dropping her purse into the front of the cart, Jill pushed it into the store.

Right off the bat, Jill noticed how bulky the Food Mart shopping carts were. Her cart was much larger than the carts she was used to using at Hal's Market. Judging by the handful of families with kids standing in the basket part of the cart, she figured this was a good thing—there was no way these carts were going to tip on accident. Still, she had to refrain from stepping in and saying anything when she passed by one child who was jumping up and shaking the sides of the cart in an attempt to get his mother's attention. Didn't any of these families know how dangerous this was? Didn't they know her son had died just a few months earlier just from standing in the cart? But the carts were large enough that they hardly wobbled from the abuse they were being put through.

The aisles at Food Mart were anything but large, despite the bulky nature of the carts. Jill's trepidation over being inside a store again grew into frustration as she navigated the constricted pathways. However, her annoyance wasn't shared. The narrow aisles seemed to be widely accepted as everyone moved in one uniform line down the aisles.

Jill became even more frustrated when she found herself stuck behind a family with a little boy intent on throwing the items from his cart onto the floor. At first Jill retrieved every item, handing them to the tired mom who appeared oblivious to her son's escapade. It was much to the amusement of the little boy. He eyed Jill with a mischievous look, throwing more and more things in her path. Jill finally caught on to the game and gave up on the retrieval. She stepped by each tiny land bomb he threw on the laminated floor, skirting around the cereal boxes and fruit snacks in her path.

Eventually the boy grew bored of his vacated audience and began knocking boxes off the shelves to occupy himself. This finally caught the attention of his mother, and she stopped the cart to give him a firm lecture. All Jill was able to do was stop with them, blocked on both sides and unable to move forward or backward. The entrance to the aisle was only a few feet away, and the woman's cart blocked the line forming behind her. Jill inched her cart forward, hoping the mother would get the hint. She didn't. Even though Jill knew she shouldn't try to squeeze by, she decided to try anyway. Her cart scraped the other one loudly, and both the mother and son turned to stare at her. Jill offered an apologetic smile even though she didn't feel sorry in the least, ignoring the angry glare the woman gave her in return. However, the woman still moved her cart forward, allowing Jill the room to escape the gridlock and disappear down the next aisle.

With her cart still empty, Jill could tell this shopping trip was going to last forever unless she came up with some sort of game plan. She glanced around the store in an attempt to make sense of the unfamiliar layout. She then perused the outskirts of the aisles, parking her cart at the end of each one, then darting back and forth as she gathered the items Michael had listed for her. Soon she was navigating the store like an old pro. She was so engrossed in crossing items off of her list, that she almost didn't see the dark-haired girl kneeling near the cheese until she was almost on top of her. Jill pulled her cart back with a lurch to avoid hitting her at the same time the girl stood up, placing her hands protectively on her swollen belly. She appeared to be only a teenager despite her pregnant condition, and she let out a nervous giggle when she realized she'd escaped being run over.

"Sorry," the girl said, lowering her eyes and grabbing a package of string cheese before moving out of the way

"No, *I'm* sorry," Jill said. "I should have been paying attention. Are you okay?"

"I'm fine," the girl muttered, tucking a piece of hair behind her ear. She leaned to the side to pick up the hand basket near her feet, then shot Jill a sheepish smile as she walked around her.

Jill parked her cart and moved in front of it as she studied the cheeses on the refrigerated shelves. She then glanced at the list in her hand. Michael had only listed "cheese," never specifying what type he wanted.

Sometimes he liked cheddar, other times he wanted Monterey jack. Rather than guess, she decided maybe to give him a call and find out for sure. But when she looked toward her purse where her phone was, she froze. So did the young pregnant girl who was clutching the purse's strap.

"What are you doing?" Jill demanded. The girl sprang back, yanking the purse with her. But she lost her grip and dropped it, the contents spilling across the linoleum. The girl grabbed the wallet from the scattered belongings, and then ran. "Stop!" Jill called out. She let go of the cheese and dropped to the floor to try and gather her belongings, but realized that by doing so, she was letting the girl get away. She abandoned her purse and the cart in an effort to catch the girl. Shoppers stepped to the side as the two women ran through the store, but no one stepped in to help. "She has my wallet!" Jill cried out as they reached the cash registers. She only caught a glimpse of the shocked cashier's face as they ran past and out the front doors.

For being pregnant, the girl was surprisingly nimble. Jill panted as she tried not to lose sight of her. She could see the girl headed for a car with an open door, panicking when she realized she might not catch her in time. It wasn't the money she was worried about, though the loss of $200 in cash and all her credit cards was definitely going to sting. But all Jill could think of were the few photos of Toby she kept tucked between the folds—photos she didn't have replacements for. If she let this girl get away, she'd never see those versions of his smile again.

This realization gave Jill the stamina to push harder against the pavement until she was in a full sprint. The girl took one last look over her shoulder as Jill closed in and grabbed her shoulder. The girl yanked away, but ended up tripping over her own feet. Without thinking, Jill lunged forward and caught her, twisting her body so she'd be the one to absorb the fall instead of the girl's belly. The girl cried out when they hit the cement, and Jill felt something in her arm snap, sending a bolt of electricity through her shoulder and sparking in her head. She let go of the girl and huddled into a shaking ball, whimpering against the severe pain of the fracture. The girl moved, still holding on to the wallet. But Jill caught a glimmer of concern cross her face. For a moment, Jill was certain she'd drop the wallet, maybe even help her. But the look was erased as soon as it came, replaced by a look of determination. The girl was now free to get away, it being apparent that Jill wasn't going to come after her.

"Get in the car, Maddie," a gruff voice called from the car. The girl scrambled to her feet, clutching the wallet to her belly, and scrambled to the car. But the cashier, the one Jill had called to, grabbed the girl from behind before she could escape.

"Watch it! I'm pregnant!" the girl yelled, but the cashier held on. Police sirens could be heard in the distance. Jill remained on the ground, closing her eyes against the agony radiating from her arm. "Wait!" she heard the girl scream. Jill could recognize the panic in her voice. She opened her eyes just in time to see the car that had been waiting for the girl speed away, the door still open and its tires squealing as the driver peeled out of the parking lot.

"Ma'am, are you okay?" a man asked her. He knelt beside her and rested his hand on her shoulder. Despite it being her unhurt arm, Jill still winced.

"I think…" she began, her emotions catching up with her now that someone was helping her. "I think I broke my arm," she said, and dissolved into a mess of tears. The throbbing in her arm had now spread to her entire body. She couldn't move anything without the pain shuddering through her. "And my purse, and my shopping cart," she whimpered.

"We'll find it for you," the man said. Jill could now see the badge on his jacket that announced he was the manager of the store. He reached up behind her and then held up the wallet that was handed to him by the cashier and then pressed it into her free hand. She grasped it close to her, squeezing her eyes shut in both relief and agony. "We've called an ambulance, and it will be here shortly. Can I call anyone else for you?" he asked.

"My husband, please," she said, wincing. He pulled a cellphone out of his pocket and dialed the numbers Jill recited for him.

Jill watched the girl as a police officer sat her on the ground near the wall, peppering her with questions. She could tell that the girl wasn't cooperating by the frustration in the officer's stance. However, she didn't miss the guilt that flashed across the girl's face as their eyes met. Jill saw the girl as she was—a wild child who had probably run away from home after getting knocked up. But there seemed to be something else there, too—a sense of desperation in her eyes that Jill wasn't able to ignore. In spite of the situation, Jill felt a sense of compassion toward the girl.

The ambulance came just as the police officers helped the handcuffed girl to her feet. Two paramedics stepped out of the vehicle, and Jill caught her breath at the similarity of the scene. *It's different, though. It's not the same.* They helped her onto a gurney and wheeled her toward the ambulance. Jill could see the police officer placing his hand on the girl's head as he seated her in the back seat of the patrol car. That was the last thing she saw as the gurney entered the back of the vehicle. The doors closed, and Jill closed her eyes as well. And on the short ride to the hospital, she got more sleep than she had in months.

Maddie Russo

~ Four ~
Not Our Little Girl

Maddie ducked her head down under the pressure of the officer's hand, giving up all efforts of the fight she'd had in her just moments before. What was the point? They had her. At least she'd have a warm place to sleep tonight.

She could have killed Jordan, even as she understood why he took off and let her bear the full brunt of his scheme. It had all seemed so simple when he had relayed the plan. Who would suspect a pregnant girl to do anything against the law? Despite her growing belly and disheveled hair, she still possessed the look of a girl who came from a good home. With her wide brown eyes and effortless smile, she had the face of innocence.

But inside, she held the rage of a girl who had been turned out by her parents once the pregnancy test came back positive...

One month earlier in Gallup, New Mexico.

"But where am I supposed to go?" Maddie cried.

"Why don't you go find that low-life boyfriend of yours and tell him you're his problem now," her father said. He stood firm, his military background shining through as he looked at his daughter without any hint of sympathy. Even though it had been years since he'd retired from the Army, he still sported the close cropped hair and muscular build. And Maddie, she was expected to be his little soldier, standing in line and only doing as told.

"Bill, please," her mother said, placing her hand on her husband's arm. As large and intimidating as Maddie's father was, her mother was the exact opposite. Petite in every sense of the word, her mother took to sweaters and pearls, her light brown hair always combed and pulled back. She aimed for perfection, volunteered for the PTA, and attended Bible studies in the middle of the week. Maddie's mom was firm in her beliefs, and consistent in her appearance. But she always stood down when it came to Maddie's dad. So when her mom tried to stop him with the touch of her hand, Maddie wasn't surprised to see him shake her off and turn his glare toward her.

"Not now, Carol. Maddie needs to learn she can't just go around life doing whatever she damn well pleases with no repercussions whatsoever," he said.

"But she's pregnant. We can't just throw her out," her mother pleaded.

"She should have thought about that before sleeping around. We've raised our children."

"But this will be our grandchild!" her mom argued.

Maddie's dad was silent for a moment as he regarded his wife. For a moment, Maddie thought he might reconsider. But when her father returned his cold gaze to her, Maddie's heart fell.

"No it won't," her father said. "Because I don't have a daughter."

The words struck Maddie, taking her breath away. She could feel the tears hovering in her eyes, but she willed them to stay back. She closed her mouth, setting it into a firm line as she worked to mirror the icy stare of her father.

"Fine," she said. She turned on her heel and went to walk toward her bedroom.

"Where do you think you're going, young lady?" her father called behind her.

"I'm going to get my things," she muttered through clenched teeth.

"What?"

"I'm going to get my things!" she yelled, turning to face him with her hands on her hips. Her father only glared at her.

"You don't have any things," he told her.

"Yes I do!" she yelled. She could feel her chest burning as her fury erupted in the hallway. Her father remained calm.

"No, you don't," he said. "I bought all those things. They're mine."

"You didn't buy everything!" Maddie yelled. "What about all of my Christmas presents? And what the hell are you going to do with all my clothing, my stuffed animals, and the pictures of all my friends?" she demanded.

"Whatever the hell I want," he replied with narrowed eyes.

Maddie took several deep breaths as she faced her father, every muscle in her body clenched. She waited for him to back down, to tell her he'd give her another chance, to let her know he was only teaching her a lesson, and the lesson was now over. But he never did. Instead, he moved to the side and pointed toward the door as if she were a mere dog being ordered outside.

She thought of all the things in her room she was leaving behind. Her pillow, the one she'd both laughed and cried into. Her favorite sweatshirt, the light pink one with the hood. The teddy bear she'd had since the day she was born. The dozens of photos that lined her mirror, reminding her of friends she had once been close to before she met Jordan. Her journal that detailed every single one of her thoughts, including thoughts she never wanted her parents to know.

"You don't own my journal," she said. "I'm getting my journal."

Her father regarded her for a moment, then nodded his head toward her bedroom.

"Fine," he said. "But you have two minutes, or I'll come in there and throw you out myself."

Maddie didn't hesitate. She turned on her heel and rushed into her room. She opened the drawer next to her bed and pulled out the journal and a pen. She also grabbed the small stash of money she'd been putting aside for a rainy day, stuffing the dollars in her pocket. She looked around the room, searching for anything else she could grab. After a moment's thought, she took her pink sweatshirt out of her drawer and slipped it on. Then she grabbed her backpack and began stuffing whatever clothes she could find that would accommodate her soon-to-be-growing body.

"No!" her father yelled, standing in the doorway. "Drop the bag and get out." He strode forward, and Maddie clutched the bag to her chest, ready to fight him if she had to.

"No, Bill," her mother said, determination in her voice. She held on to his arm tight, and didn't let go when he tried to shake her off. "It's bad enough that she has to leave. The least we can do is to let her go with a few things."

"The least we could do was everything we already did— raise her with proper ideals, a roof over her head, and with all that we worked hard for so that she could live a good life," he hissed. But he didn't fight his wife, allowing Maddie the time to pull her backpack on and grab her journal off the bed. Eyeing her dad, she also grabbed the teddy bear off of her pillow. Without a word, she dared him to stop her. He didn't.

Maddie looked at her mom. Tears were now streaming from her mother's eyes down her cheeks. She rushed forward and grabbed Maddie into a bear hug.

"I'm so sorry, honey," she said. She pushed something into Maddie's hand away from the hovering eyes of her husband. Maddie recognized the familiar texture of dollar bills, and she quickly stuffed them into her pocket with the rest of her money. She knew this wasn't her mother's decision for her to go. Still, she kept her emotions from spilling over. Her mom could stop all of this from happening. She could put her foot down. But she didn't this time, just like she never stood up to Maddie's dad every other time he laid down the law.

It was Maddie who pulled away from the embrace first, and her mom put her hand over her mouth with a sob. Without saying a word, Maddie strode past her parents and out of the room, down the hall and through the front door for the very last time. It wasn't until she'd hit the sidewalk when the sound of her mother's sobbing stopped following her. And still, she knew that sound would haunt her for a very long time.

Gallup, New Mexico was known for its arid weather. This day was no different. The walk to Jordan's house was long on the hot, summer day. Maddie pulled the sweatshirt over her head, stuffing it, the journal, and her teddy bear all into the already limited space of the backpack. She searched her pocket for her cellphone, and swore when she realized she had left it on the kitchen counter where she'd placed it before telling her parents she was pregnant. It didn't matter anyway, her dad would most likely have had it shut off by now. But now she couldn't call Jordan to come pick her up. She was just glad she was wearing tennis shoes instead of heels when she was forced to leave.

Reality was starting to sink in about her predicament. She could never go home. Maddie wiped her moistened eyes on the hem of her shirt repeatedly, trying to rid herself of the tears that wouldn't stop. She was angry that her dad could actually turn his back on her. And she was also devastated. She didn't know what she was doing, or how to be a mother. How was she going to do this without her mom?

It was nearly thirty minutes later when she reached the walkway to Jordan's house. He lived on a crowded street where the lawns were never mowed and people actually parked their cars in their front yards. It was a stark difference from Maddie's manicured neighborhood, where neighbors sent nasty letters if the trash cans were left out a day too long. Here, even the chipped paint on every house was looking for a way out.

Maddie took a deep breath and let it out slow, even though she'd been to Jordan's house a hundred times before. This time was different. Would he take her in? Did she even want to stay here? She hated Jordan's parents, and his house was a wreck. But did she have any other choice? She didn't. Mustering up her courage, she raised her hand and knocked on the door.

Jordan answered, wearing a pair of jeans and a white tank top that revealed his tanned arms covered in a map of colorful tattoos. He smiled when he saw Maddie, though she could see the question in his face, his square jawline tensing as he eyed her backpack slung over her shoulder.

"They kicked me out," she blurted out. She gauged his reaction, watching carefully to see how he'd handle the weight of this news. When a flash of disappointment crossed his unshaven face, however, she dismissed it as quickly as he did.

"Looks like you're staying here, then, aren't you?" he said, pulling her into a bear hug. She sighed, burying her face into his chest and inhaling. He smelled of cigarettes, beer, and security. "Don't worry, Maddie. Everything's going to be okay," he said into her hair. Then he pulled away and grinned down on her. "Besides, now I get you all to myself forever." She grinned back at him, tucking her uneasiness and feelings of abandonment aside as he leaned down and took her by the mouth, giving her a long kiss. Jordan wanted her, even if her parents tossed her aside. "Come on," he murmured against her lips. "Let's get you inside."

It took a few moments for Maddie's eyes to adjust to the darkness of the house. Once Jordan closed the door, the only sources of light came from the glow of the TV in the corner of the living room and the hint of sunshine that escaped from behind the closed blinds. The air inside was stale, stuffy from the smoke cloud that seemed to hover in the middle of the living room. Maddie longed for an open window, seeking fresh air with each breath.

"Mom, Dad, Maddie's staying with us for a while," Jordan announced to the room. Maddie's eyes adjusted to the dim light. She could see Jordan's mom sleeping on the couch, her hair still in pink curlers, and her slender frame wrapped in a ratty blue robe. Jordan's dad was sitting in his arm chair, just as he always did when she came by. He was wearing the same red flannel shirt he'd worn the last two times she's been over, his belly poking out in the strained spaces between the buttons. A beer rested in his hand, and a cigarette dangled from his mouth. He turned toward them upon Jordan's announcement, looking Maddie up and down. She resisted the urge to shudder, inching closer to Jordan instead.

"Hey, girlie," his dad offered as his greeting. Maddie nodded, giving a quick smile.

"Hi Mr. and Mrs. Turner," she said.

"Now, you know better than that," he said. "It's Stan. And that lump over there is Irene. None of this Mr. and Mrs. crap."

"Um, okay…Stan," Maddie said. He just nodded, and turned back to his TV.

Jordan led Maddie to his room—her room now, too. He took her bag from her shoulder and placed it on the floor. Maddie looked around the cramped space. With the door closed, it made the room feel even smaller. Without a bedframe, Jordan's mattress lay on the floor, a pile of tangled blankets and sheets on top. The room held the same smoky smell as the rest of the house, which Maddie contributed to the filled ashtray on the dresser near Jordan's bed. The closet was open, a few empty hangers existing between Jordan's shirts and pants. Maddie opened her bag and pulled out the clothes she had grabbed from her house, hanging them beside his clothes in the closet.

"Just like being home, right?" Jordan chuckled. Maddie laughed with him. It wasn't like being at home at all. But still, she couldn't stop the excited flutter in her belly just thinking about staying here with Jordan, spending the night with him every night.

That excitement didn't last long.

Jordan left early the next morning for work, leaving Maddie to figure out her own day without him. She laid there in bed, trying to think of all the things she could do now that she was no longer under her parent's thumb. But nothing came to mind. None of her things were here, she didn't really know Jordan's parents very well, and she wasn't sure what she was allowed to eat or not. She stared up at the ceiling for more than an hour until her bladder couldn't take any more. Slipping on a robe, she padded to the door and eased it open. From the other end of the hall she could hear the muffled sounds of Jordan's parents talking. No, they were fighting, she realized, recognizing the urgent tone in their voices. Stan's deeper voice rose in volume as Irene shrieked in between loud sobs. Maddie slipped into the bathroom and closed the door behind her, hoping she could finish and disappear again before they emerged from the room and filled the house with the awkward knowledge that she knew they were arguing.

They were still fighting when she was done, and Maddie tiptoed back to Jordan's room on the balls of her feet. But her grumbling belly made her change course. *Maybe I can just grab something from the fridge before they come out.* She hurried to the kitchen and was disgusted by her surroundings. The sink was filled with dirty dishes. It appeared no one had washed any in days, maybe longer. The floor was sticky against Maddie's bare feet, and she continued on tiptoe to avoid dirtying her feet any more than she had to. Opening the fridge, she found shelves full of condiments and beer, a loaf of bread, and a carton of eggs. She looked behind her at the dirty kitchen, trying to figure out how she could make herself something to eat without a clean pan in sight. Sighing, she realized she couldn't.

"This is my home now, too" she muttered, surveying the kitchen as she guessed how long it would take to clean. She set to work, rolling up the sleeves of her bathrobe and emptying the sink of dishes. She scrubbed the sink, and then filled it with water. Then she did the dishes in shifts—starting with plates, then cups, then silverware, and finally, the pans. It took more than thirty minutes, the soundtrack of Jordan's parents fighting in the background. When the dishes were all dried and put away, she wiped down the counters, then swept the floor with a broom she found in a closet. She couldn't find a mop, so she wet a cloth with soap and water, and took to scrubbing the floor little by little on her hands and knees.

It wasn't till she was halfway through with the floor when she realized the house was silent. Maddie glanced over her shoulder, her heart leaping in her chest when she saw Stan at the edge of the kitchen, watching her with a glazed expression on his face.

"Oh, sorry," he muttered, snapping back to attention and flashing her an apologetic grin. "I didn't mean to startle you."

"It's okay, Mr. Turner," Maddie said, bracing herself as she stood up on the wet floor, pulling the sash of her robe a little tighter.

"Now, don't make me reprimand you," Jordan's dad said. Maddie looked at him quizzically, and he winked at her. "It's Stan, remember?" he said. Maddie gave him a sheepish grin.

"Okay…Stan," she said to him. Stan looked around the kitchen and gave a low whistle.

"Well, you've been busy, I see," he said, nodding in approval. Maddie blushed, but smiled at the recognition. At home, her parents never noticed anything she did— only when she failed to do her chores in a timely manner. "Looks nice," he said. Her blush deepened under the compliment.

"Thank you, Mr., er, Stan. It's nothing really. I was just hungry and saw that there wasn't anything clean. I mean…. Sorry, I didn't mean it that way." Maddie wanted to disappear into the floor she had almost finished mopping. But Stan just shook his head.

"No, it's okay. It was a real big mess. But it seems that Irene has forgotten how to clean," he glowered. "Seems Irene has forgotten how to do anything around here!" he shouted toward the back of the house. A door slammed, and Maddie winced at the sound, as well as at Stan's words.

"Mr. Turner," Maddie pleaded, reverting back to his formal name. Stan looked at her, the anger evident in his eyes. But he softened his gaze once again.

"Sorry," he said. "I guess you probably already knew me and the missus were fighting, though."

"No," Maddie lied. But then she realized how obvious it was that she had. "I mean, yes, I heard you and Mrs…Irene fighting. But everyone gets into fights now and then." She hoped he bought it. Her parents never fought. Her father just said how things were supposed to go, and her mom went along with it. Until yesterday, she hadn't ever seen her parents argue about anything.

But Stan just shook his head.

"Not like us," he muttered. "It's just, that woman! All she does is drink, sleep, and tell me how much she hates me. And it's not like she's any kind of catch herself. She won't work, she leaves the house looking like this," he swept his hand around them, "and she doesn't look...well, she doesn't look like you."

Maddie shrank back at his words, her cheeks burning as he looked at her.

"I mean...I just mean she doesn't take care of herself like you do," he countered. "I mean, you must work out, or something."

"Um, no," Maddie stuttered. She wondered how much Jordan had told his parents about her condition. She decided to take a chance, hoping it meant he'd stop looking at her the way he still was. "I don't want to do anything that might hurt the baby."

"The baby," he repeated. The look in Stan's eyes changed to confusion for a moment, and then switched to shock in the next. "Oh! A baby!" Maddie caught a glimmer of disappointment cross his face before he flashed her a grin. "Well, congratulations," he told her. "The boy done good." He winked at her with the last statement, and Maddie refrained from shuddering as she smiled.

"Thanks," she said. Her stomach rumbled, loud enough for even Stan to take notice.

"Was that you?" he asked with a laugh. She gave an embarrassed laugh and nodded. "You haven't eaten yet, have you?" he asked.

"No sir," she said. He walked past her and opened the fridge, peering in at its meager contents.

"Not much in there, unless you want beer and eggs," he said.

"There's bread in there, too," she said. "I was just going to make some eggs and toast."

"Don't be silly," he said. "You're eating for two now."

"Eggs and toast is a perfectly normal breakfast," Maddie pointed out.

"Yes, but what are you going to eat for lunch?" he asked. Maddie didn't answer. "It's settled. Go get dressed, I'm taking you to breakfast, and then we're going shopping."

"But what about Irene?" Maddie asked.

"She likes beer. Let her drink that."

- Five -
Running Free

Maddie sat at the table in the center of The Pancake House, an empty plate in front of her and her belly feeling fuller than usual. She rested her hand on her stomach. She had only just started showing, but now her belly felt inflated from the way she inhaled her breakfast.

"Get enough?" Stan asked from across the table. She'd only had two pancakes and a side of fruit, but it was enough to send her over the edge. He, on the other hand, had managed to polish off a stack of pancakes, along with four slabs of bacon, some sausage, and a mound of scrambled eggs.

"Yes, thank you, Stan," she said, sitting back with a sigh and a smile for emphasis. Stan waved down the waitress for the check, then paid without looking like he even gave it a second thought. Without any evidence of income, Maddie wondered how he was able to pay. She dismissed the thought as soon as it came. *Not my business...*

"Time for the store?" he asked. Maddie gave him a shy smile. There was no food in the house. If they didn't go to the store, she wasn't sure what she was going to eat after this meal. But she also knew he was only doing this because of her.

"You don't need to go to all this trouble," she insisted.

"Nonsense. We all need to eat, right?" Maddie nodded. "Then let's get out of here."

Once at the store, Stan let Maddie take the lead. At first, she was modest in her choices. She tried to think like her mother, choosing practical foods over the higher calorie convenience meals. But when she noticed Stan fumbling with the packages of fresh chicken and ground beef, she realized they might not be so practical in this household. She got the impression that Irene didn't know how to cook, and with the way Stan was looking at each item she suggested, he didn't seem like much of a cook, either. Maddie also didn't have much experience with the stove, her mother always being the one to fix the family's meals. And Jordan? She was certain he'd never picked up a frying pan in his life. A household of four non-cooks. It was a safe bet that any fresh food they bought now was just going to go to waste.

"You know what? I've changed my mind on those," Maddie said to Stan as he began to place a bag of potatoes in the cart. The relief on his face was unmistakable.

"What would you like instead?" he asked. Together, they returned all the items they'd collected back to their rightful shelves, and then grabbed new food choices from the frozen foods aisle. The cart was near full by the time they were done, and Stan pulled a wad of cash from his wallet when the cashier gave him the total. Maddie couldn't help staring at the money in his hand, but looked away when he glanced at her. When she looked back at him, he just gave her a wink.

Once home, she helped him to unload all the groceries. There almost wasn't enough room in the freezer, but Stan made things fit by taking a few meals out of their boxes and shoving them in between packages.

"We'll just have to guess how long to microwave them for," he laughed.

When the last was put away, he turned and gave her a triumphant grin and a thumbs up. Maddie was starting to forget her first impressions of him, and grinned back at him. Maybe he wasn't so bad, after all.

"Are you hungry?" he asked. She shook her head. The pancake breakfast still lay heavy on her stomach, and the thought of eating didn't interest her at all. Stan pulled one of the unpackaged meals out of the freezer and turned on the oven. There didn't seem to be any reason to stick around, so Maddie moved to go back to Jordan's bedroom.

"Wait, where are you going?" Stan asked. Maddie paused, turning back toward him.

"I just thought I'd take a nap," she lied.

"You don't have to go," he said. "Why don't you stay awhile?" He pulled out a seat at the kitchen table and patted it. Something in his smile made her feel uneasy. She shook her head.

"I'm sorry, Stan," she said. "I'm just so tired. I think it's the pregnancy and all, I get worn out so much easier these days." She waited for him to argue with her, but he just smiled and nodded.

"Fair enough. Thank you for cleaning up and helping me shop," he said.

"You're welcome. Thank you for breakfast." She left him in the kitchen, closing the door behind her once she was in the bedroom.

The bed was still unmade from the morning, and her robe lay across the floor. She had never been one for neatness at her own house. But being in a home where cleanliness didn't matter, she found the urge to keep the spaces around her tidy. She did a quick run through of Jordan's room—making the bed, picking up her clothes, and straightening a few items Jordan had left out. One of them was an interesting wooden box that lay open on the floor. Maddie picked it up, admiring the detail in the carvings on the outside before placing it on his nightstand.

When the room was clean, she looked through a pile of books in Jordan's closet. He didn't have many to choose from, so she just grabbed the one that looked the most interesting. She settled into his bed and opened the book. The story was about an English man who lost his identity and found himself in a strange new world under the streets of London. The story was interesting enough, but after an hour of reading, she found herself fighting against the heaviness of her eyelids. Maddie marked her place in the book and laid it on the pillow next to her. Then she rolled over and closed her eyes.

She'd just drifted off when she heard a click. Her eyes flew open, and she gasped when she saw Stan leaning against the closed bedroom door.

"Don't say anything," he said quietly, and he moved to the bed. Maddie scrambled to sit up, but he landed on top of her. "You don't want to alarm Irene, or you'll be in a lot of trouble," he whispered in her ear, his breath already laden with the scent of alcohol. He didn't elaborate who she'd be in trouble with, and Maddie was afraid to ask.

"Mr. Turner, please," she whimpered. Stan fumbled with the covers, pulling at them until they fell to the floor, stripping her of one more barrier between them, as well as any caution of being in trouble with him or Irene. "Mr. Turner, stop!" she screamed. She fought against him, twisting underneath him and kneeing him in the groin. He groaned, rolling off her and curling into a ball. Maddie scrambled from the bed and lunged at the door. But in an instant, Stan was off the bed, grabbing her by the hair and pulling her back. Maddie yelped as he flung her back on the mattress and began pawing at her clothes. She tried to push his heavy body off of her, but was no match against his weight. Stan mashed his hand over her mouth as she tried once again to scream. She couldn't understand why Irene wasn't hearing any of the struggle. Tears squeezed from Maddie's eyes as Stan ripped her shirt, shedding it from her body. Her teeth found his hand and she bit down, tasting his blood in her mouth. Stan cried out, removing his hand for a moment. But before she could scream for help, he smacked her across the face.

"Stop making this difficult," he hissed at her, then forced her on to her belly as he fumbled with her pants. Maddie gasped for breath as her face was mashed into her pillow, and she tried to claw herself away. It was no use.

He had his hand firmly on the back of her head, keeping her pressed against the pillow with no way to get air, every bit of her struggle stealing the little breath she had left. Maddie grew lightheaded, giving in to the fight. But then she felt Stan's weight lift off her body, leaving her alone on the mattress. She rolled over, covering her bare chest with her arms as Jordan threw his father on the floor and punched him in the face.

"Jordan," she gasped. He continued to punch his father repeatedly, one hit after another as Stan covered his face in protection.

"What were you thinking!?" Jordan growled, grabbing his dad by the shirt and lifting him so that his face was an inch away. Stan took the opportunity to head-butt his son, scrambling out from under him as Jordan reeled back. He lunged for the door, but Jordan recovered and pulled him back. Maddie could see the veins in Jordan's neck and the muscles bulging in his arms as Jordan opened the door and threw his father to the ground in the hallway.

Maddie jumped off the bed, grabbing a t-shirt from the floor and pulling it on. She raced into the living room as Jordan stood over his father. Irene lay on the couch, rousing as if she had just woken from a nap.

"Where were you when my girlfriend was being attacked by your husband?" Jordan yelled at her.

"What?" she slurred. Maddie could see the beginnings of a bruise forming on Irene's cheek as she lifted her head and looked around. There was the unmistakable hint of recognition in Irene's eyes, as if she had known what was going on the whole time.

"You heard me. Why didn't you stop him?" Jordan growled. He clenched and unclenched his fists, and for a moment Maddie was afraid he was going to go after his mother, too.

"Jordan," Maddie whispered. He turned and looked at her, the rage in his eyes landing on her. Maddie cowered back against the wall, unsure if he was angry with her, too, when his gaze didn't soften. Jordan turned back to his parents.

"You disgust me," he sneered at both of them, then turned to walk away. His father scrambled to his feet, ready to pounce.

"Jordan!" Maddie screamed. Jordan turned and landed on his father with a straight punch to the jaw. Stan landed on his back, stunned. He rolled to his side, protecting himself. But Jordan didn't continue. He just got up and strode past Maddie into the room.

"Come on, Maddie. We're getting out of here," he said, his jaw set as he pulled a bag from the closet and began throwing both of their clothes in it. He went to the dresser by the bed, but then froze when he saw the box sitting on top of it. "Where did you get this," he asked Maddie, going over to it and picking it up.

"It was on the floor," she whispered. "I just set it there when I was straightening up." His tone scared her, and her hands shook as he opened it up, swearing under his breath when he saw that it was empty.

"Where's the money?" he demanded.

"I don't know what you're talking about," Maddie said. "It was empty when I found it, I swear."

"Where's my money!" Jordan yelled, storming out of the room and back in the living room. Stan still lay on the floor, but Maddie could see his smirk from the bedroom.

"The groceries," she said, realizing where Stan had gotten all the money. Jordan looked back at her, then marched into the kitchen. She scrambled after him, entering the room as he stared at the open refrigerator full of food.

"You used all my money on food!" he yelled.

"We have to eat, Jordan. It's only fair, anyway, since you brought another mouth into this house to feed," his father called from the living room. Maddie stepped aside as Jordan strode back into the living room.

"Jordan, let's just go," Maddie pleaded. He turned to her and glared.

"We don't have any money, Maddie," he hissed.

"I have money," she told him. She went into the room and pulled open the drawer to the dresser on her side of the bed. The journal still lay there, and she pulled it out. She opened it up, breathing a sigh of relief that the money was still there. She picked it out of the pages and held it out to Jordan. "My mom gave me a little before I left, and I had some saved up, too. It's not much, but it's enough. Let's just go."

Jordan regarded the money for a moment. Then he gave Maddie a slight nod. He took the money from her, and then picked up the bag of their things off the bed.

"Come on," he said to Maddie, leading her to the door.

"Wait, where are you going?" Irene said, raising her head off the couch. Jordan ignored her and reached for the door. Maddie looked back at Irene, noting the alarm in her eyes as she suddenly realized what was happening. "Jordan!" his mother screamed.

"Pipe down, Irene. Let the boy go," Maddie heard Stan say as she followed Jordan down the front steps to his car in the driveway.

Once in the car, Jordan gunned the engine before putting it into reverse. Irene streaked out of the house, waving her arms wildly as they pulled onto the street. Maddie couldn't help feeling sorry for the woman, noting the anguish in her eyes as it became apparent they were really leaving. She also couldn't keep the jealousy from rolling in, remembering how her own mother didn't even try to stop her from leaving. Maddie watched as the view of Jordan's mother got smaller and smaller in the rear window. Then she was gone.

Maddie turned back around, looking at the road that lay ahead. She leaned against the door to rest. She wasn't sure where they were going. She wasn't even convinced Jordan knew either. But in the moment, she felt freer than she ever had before.

~ Six ~
We're Not in Gallup Anymore

Jordan drove for just over three hours before the fuel gauge teetered on empty. He pulled into the gas station as Maddie fought sleep with her head against the window. Emblazoned in bright letters on the mini market was "Flagstaff Market." They had reached Arizona.

It was just past six o'clock, hardly late by any means. But Maddie still felt wiped. The baby was taking so much of her energy lately, and now was no exception. Even just sitting in the passenger seat felt exhausting. Still, she knew she needed to stretch her legs and relieve her bladder while she still could. So she opened the door and got out, giving Jordan a quick peck as he filled up the tank.

"Could you get me a soda while you're in there?" he asked her, and she nodded, taking the few dollars he handed her.

The bathroom smelled strongly of urine and cheap cleaning solution. Maddie tried not to touch anything in the room, washing her hands thoroughly when she was finished. She looked in the mirror, peering at the dark circles under her eyes and her messy hair. It had only been one day since she left her home to move in with Jordan. Still, it felt like a lifetime ago since she had lived in a cozy house in Gallup, her every need taken care of by her parents. Now here she was, on the road with a dwindling wad of cash, her destination as mysterious as the town they had just stopped in. Where would they end up? Would they even have enough to get there? Maddie felt her heart race as she reviewed all the changes they were facing with no plan in place. Jordan had left his job. She was abandoning her childhood town. They had no place to sleep, no food to eat. And the way the gas needle was moving, their money would run out sometime the next day.

Afraid to spend the few dollars in her hand, Maddie walked back to the car without ever stopping to grab Jordan a soda. He gave her a quizzical look when she sat down in the passenger seat and handed back the money.

"We don't have enough for soda," she told him, determined not to back down even when his eyes narrowed.

"We have enough," Jordan insisted. "And I need to stay awake if we're going to keep driving."

"But you're already filling up the gas tank after only three hours of driving," Maddie argued. She turned to peer at how much the gas had cost them, and winced when she saw it said $43.57. "Where are we going, Jordan? And how are we going to have enough to get there?"

Jordan didn't speak right away. At first, Maddie thought he was angry at her for asking too many questions. But then she could see the brooding look in his eyes.

"I'm not sure," he admitted. "I have a few options, but I haven't decided what's best. And look, I hear your concern about the money. I'm concerned, too. But I have a few more tricks up my sleeve, so don't you worry." He leaned over and kissed her cheek, taking his hand and squeezing her thigh in reassurance. Despite her fears, Maddie decided it was easier just to trust him, believing that he knew what he was doing and everything would be okay.

"All right," she told him. He grinned at her and gave her a wink.

"I'm going to go in and get myself a soda," he told her, patting her thigh when she opened her mouth to protest. "It's just a few dollars, and I need to keep myself awake."

"Fine," Maddie conceded. "But just a soda."

Jordan disappeared for a few minutes, then returned holding a small bag. Maddie could feel the heat rising in her cheeks as he sat down and handed her a soda for herself before emptying the contents of the bag on the seat—a map, a pack of cigarettes, and a bag of chips.

"Jordan, we don't have enough for this!" she insisted. Maddie could feel hot tears filling her eyes as she clenched and unclenched her hands in frustration.

"I told you, Maddie, I have a plan. We'll be just fine."

Jordan pulled out of the gas station and continued driving down the I-40. Still fuming, Maddie kept her focus on the scenery as they drove, watching the desert whip by them from her window so that it was one reddish brown blur, the Arizona sun descending toward the horizon. Her stomach grumbled, and she gave in to taking a few chips from the bag that lay between them, washing it down with the soda in her hand.

"See? It's not so bad, right babe?" Jordan asked. Maddie ignored him and continued to look out the window. But soon she had to speak up again, her bladder feeling like it was close to bursting.

"Again?" he asked.

"I'm pregnant," she reminded him. "And I had all that soda."

They pulled into the next rest stop, and Maddie unbuckled and got out as soon as the car came to a halt. Dusk was nearing, and their surroundings took on a pink hue as she walked toward the stucco facilities. Unlike the gas station, this restroom was immaculate, save for a few dozen crickets that hopped around the concrete floor. Maddie hurried to finish, then washed the sweat and grime from traveling off her hands and face.

When she left the bathroom, she walked toward the car, pausing when she saw it was empty. She looked around and spotted Jordan across the lot, smoking a cigarette and chatting with a man as they peered at his map. They both looked up as she approached. The man nodded politely to Maddie before continuing his conversation with Jordan.

"So you'll want to keep following this stretch of highway toward Barstow, about five hours from here. Where did you say you were going?" the man asked.

"Just north of San Diego to visit some family," Jordan said. He turned to Maddie. "Why don't you wait in the car, Maddie. I don't want you and the baby near the smoke," he said as he held up the cigarette. Maddie pursed her lips, wondering what Jordan was up to. He had smoked plenty of times in the car with her sitting beside him. But instead of arguing, she turned and walked back to the car.

Jordan joined her a few minutes later. He didn't even buckle his seatbelt before putting the car in drive and peeling onto the highway.

"Babe? Where are we going? Are we really going to San Diego?" she asked.

"Not sure yet," he answered. Then he looked over at her and gave her a sly grin. He reached into his jacket pocket and pulled out a dark object, tossing it onto her lap. It was a wallet. Maddie picked it up, opening it with cautious fingers. The man they had just been talking to stared back at her through the driver's license photo.

"But how did you...?" she started, dropping the wallet back in her lap. She was afraid to touch it, as if the wallet would stain her hands with the heated guilt coursing through her body.

"Don't worry about how I got it. It's ours now. And judging by the weight of it, that dude was carrying some major cash. Probably funding his whole road trip with money, the dumbass." Jordan licked his lips, then nodded toward the wallet in Maddie's lap. "Open it up and pull out the cash. When we get further down the road you can throw the rest of it out."

Maddie's stomach churned, thinking of the guy back at the rest stop, his family now stranded without any means of paying for anything. But as she peered into the wallet, her morals were momentarily forgotten. A stack of large bills greeted her from within the fold, tucked in between credit cards and family photos. She pulled the cash out and counted it, her heart racing as she reached the final bills.

"There's over $1,000 in here!" she exclaimed, at which Jordan gave her a toothy grin. It was more money than she'd ever held in her life, and more than enough to get them where they needed to go, wherever that was.

Maddie thumbed through the photos, studying the brightness that existed in the smile on each face. There was one of the man with an attractive woman, his arm wrapped protectively around her shoulder. The next three were school photos, a boy in different stages of his life, the innocence of his face lessening slightly with each progression. In the last one, the boy looked to be about twelve. He didn't open his mouth with his smile, but the hint of laughter still existed in his eyes. Maddie couldn't help but smile back at the photo, remembering what it was like to be twelve years old, in that place between child and adult. Four years ago, she never would have guessed she'd be here now, pregnant and on the road toward a brand new life.

"San Francisco," Jordan said out of nowhere, answering Maddie's earlier question. Maddie's face lit up with a grin.

"Really?" she asked. He nodded, glancing over at her and chuckling. Maddie settled back into her seat, smiling out the car window. A big city. She had only heard of it, and knew nothing about the city except that it had the Golden Gate Bridge. But it sounded huge and expansive, busy with tons of possibility. They could get an apartment near the water and watch the boats go by from their living room. Jordan could get a mechanics job there, or maybe even a job as a carpenter. She could stay home with the baby, maybe even watch a few other babies to make some extra money. Maddie hugged herself, secretly smiling into her elbow as she thought of all that lay before them in this new city.

"I like that," she told Jordan. He took his eyes off the road just long enough to give her a wink.

"I think it will be good," he told her. "I have a buddy who lives down there. He said he'll let us crash with them until we get on our feet." Maddie's smile wavered, disappointed that it wouldn't be just the two of them. The change in her demeanor wasn't lost on Jordan. "What?" he asked her. She shook her head and smiled again.

"It's nothing, really," she said. "I just wasn't expecting to live with any of your friends." She could see his jaw tightening at her words, his eyes blazing as he kept them trained on the road.

"Maddie, what did you expect? That at a moment's notice I would have a house all lined up next to the best schools, letting you stay home while I worked all day?" Maddie's cheeks burned as she realized that was exactly what she had expected. Reality hit her hard as she remembered they were actually homeless with no clear direction. Besides the name of the city and its huge bridge, neither of them knew anything about where they were going. The city they were traveling toward might not have anything for them.

"I'm sorry," she whispered. She could feel the tears welling up in her eyes, and she turned back toward the window as they broke so Jordan couldn't see them roll down her cheeks. What had felt so hopeful just a moment earlier now seemed futile. She missed her bed, her room, her mom and dad. She missed everything that was comfortable and familiar to her. She missed feeling safe. What if she had this baby before they ever found a place to live? How would she take care of it? She sniffed as quietly as she could, feeling Jordan's eyes on the back of her head.

"Babe, don't cry. Everything's going to be fine, you'll see." She could feel him stroke her hair from behind. "Trust me, I don't want to live with anyone else, either. If I could, I'd live in a huge house with just you, enjoying the good life. But if we want to sleep with a roof over our heads, we have to crash at someone else's pad." Maddie shuddered a sigh, leaning into his hand. She turned, taking off her seatbelt so she could scoot closer to him on the bench seat. He wrapped his arm around her shoulder and squeezed. "It will all work out," he promised with a whisper and a kiss on her ear. Maddie took a deep breath in, then let it out slow. It was easier just to believe he was right.

After a few moments, she took her seat again by the door, slipping her seatbelt back on. She then rolled her window all the way down. The cool air rushed into the car, blowing her hair all around her face. She ignored the strands whipping against her cheeks, but kept her eyes focused on the terrain as they sped down the road. Everything was dark except for the surrounding area lit up by their headlights. She picked up the wallet in her lap, folding it closed on the smiling family inside. Then she threw it as hard as she could out the window. It disappeared into the pitch black of the night, taking all the happy faces with it. Then she rolled her window back up, and leaned against it to get a few hours of sleep.

~ Seven ~
The Land of Beer and Pizza

The violent shake of the car woke Maddie with a jolt. She opened her eyes, squinting them as the bright sun crested the top of hill on the horizon. A look to her left revealed an empty seat. She looked out the window of the car, trying to orient herself to where they were as she searched for Jordan's whereabouts. The car was parked on a road, the wind from passing cars shaking the vehicle each time one went by.

Jordan emerged from behind some bushes a few moments later, a cigarette dangling from his mouth as he fumbled with his pants. He caught Maddie looking at him from the passenger side of the car and gave her a lopsided grin.

"Where are we?" she asked him when he got back in the car.

"We're in Barstow, about two hours past the California border," he told her. He chuckled when her eyes widened.

"We're in California?" She was suddenly awake, the reality of their destination becoming more clear.

"Yup. You were out last night when we crossed the border. I called my buddy at a rest stop about a hundred miles back, and we're all set. We're good to go," he said, pulling her into him for a hug. She hid her face into his chest, inhaling the scent of his cologne mingling with the ashy smell of his cigarettes as she practiced keeping her grin in place. Everything would have been so perfect if they could have just found a place to stay on their own. Jordan's words rang in her ear, words that shamed her for still feeling so selfish and unrealistic. But she didn't want to share space with anyone else. It was supposed to be just Jordan and her, and eventually, their baby.

"That's fantastic," she said against his chest, her words muffled. He didn't seem to notice if anything was amiss, and squeezed her closer to him.

"All right, according to the map we have just over four hundred miles left to go, which will probably take six or seven hours. So if you need to use the restroom, now's your time," he said.

"Uh…" Maddie looked out the window toward the bush Jordan had just finished using.

"It's a nice bush," Jordan said. "But it seems to be out of toilet paper and a flusher, so be careful where you step."

It was midday when they started seeing signs telling them how many miles away San Francisco was. When the number reached one-hundred and nine miles, it began to feel like they were finally getting somewhere. But soon it felt like the longest part of the drive. Maddie's legs felt like they were going to jump out of the car in her anxiousness to just be anywhere. She no longer cared about where they were going, who they were staying with, whether they had a place to sleep, or even if she'd ever get a home-cooked meal again. She just wanted to be done with traveling for good. The road they were on held no scenery or houses. It was just one long road of desert, with the occasional gas station every forty or so miles. It was nothing like she expected California to be.

Jordan pulled over at one of the gas stations, filling up the gas tank before driving to the edge of the parking lot for a smoke. Maddie could feel the irritation welling up inside, overwhelming every one of her senses. She opened the door and slammed it, walking away from the car to stretch her legs. Jordan either took no notice of her mood, or was ignoring it. Either way, he said nothing as she walked away. Her belly ached as if she had just finished hundreds of sit-ups, and she felt like running just to remember what it was like to move more than a few inches at a time. But she didn't. Instead, she stopped at the other end of the parking lot and did a few stretches to ease her aching muscles. Looking up, she could see Jordan had finished his cigarette. He was leaning on the hood of the car, squinting in her direction under the hot sun of the afternoon. She turned to avoid his gaze, kicking the ground in frustration. She could hear the car door slam and the engine of his car start. She refused to look up, even as she heard the car idling next to her.

"Hey pretty lady, want a ride?" he flirted through the open window. She tried to fix her scowl in place and her eyes on the ground. But she couldn't keep the giggle from escaping under the weight of his unseen smile. "Come on, babe," he said. "We only have a little bit longer. Next stop is San Francisco."

Maddie sighed, dreading any more time in the car. But she slumped over to the passenger side anyway, opening the door and sitting down hard on the seat. He teased her with a few whimpering noises, and she nudged his arm. But she couldn't help but smile at his persistence to break her bad mood.

"All right," she finally relented, relaxing her tension and giving in to the final stretch of road before them. "Let's go."

It was nearing dusk when the desert disappeared. Close knit houses and apartments littered the landscape in its place. To Maddie, it was the most beautiful sight she'd seen the whole trip. It meant they were close to "home," whatever that meant. The sun was just setting when they reached the onramp leading directly into the city, casting a golden light over the maze of freeways, crowded buildings, and the influx of cars that took up every space on the road all around them. Maggie stared out her window, mesmerized by the busyness of the city. The sinking sun cast a pink glow in the sky overlooking a billion lights ahead, and she leaned forward to make out where each one came from.

Jordan exited the freeway and they drove down a street filled with billboards and tall buildings. Looking up, Maddie could see clothes hanging off railings and graffiti that appeared more like art than vandalism. The darkening sky had no effect on the activity that surrounded them. People milled along the sidewalks as if it were broad daylight, the fronts of the shops thrown wide open without a door as a barrier. It seemed the city possessed an amplified energy as crowds traveled in packs, folding into each other while going from one end of the street to the other.

They pulled over next to a Chinese bakery, and Jordan turned off the car.

"Wait here," he ordered before getting out of the car and disappearing into the bakery. Maddie fumed at being told to stay put. They were finally here in the city, an exotic place with strange smells and interesting sights, and he wanted her to stay in the car? She toyed with the idea of getting out anyway, of exploring the street they were on, or at least checking out whatever treasures the bakery beside her had to offer. However, the vastness of the city around her made her hold on to the safety within the car. Without Jordan by her side, everything just seemed a little too big to explore on her own.

For fifteen minutes, Maddie stared out the window at the bakery. Her mouth watered as she studied the breads and pastries looking back at her from the windows lined in pink paper. Eventually, Jordan emerged carrying a bag in one hand and a piece of paper in the other. He got in the car and handed Maddie the bag. She could smell the warm fragrance from whatever lay inside before even opening it. When she unfolded the paper bag and peered in, she was greeted with the warm steam of two buns. She had never smelled anything so heavenly.

"Hand me one of those, will you?" Jordan asked, pulling out of their parking spot and back on to the road. Maddie reached in and grabbed one of the buns, surprised by the weight of it when she picked it up. She handed it to him, and he tore into it. Maddie could see a hidden pocket of meat that lay inside. She pulled her own bun out of the bag, wasting no time to bite down into it.

"Oh my God," she mumbled around her food, the flavors of the meat and warm bread filling a hole inside of her she never knew existed. It was like she could breathe again.

"Right?" Jordan said with a grin. "It's like Heaven on Earth. Pork buns are where it's at when you come to the city. Ain't no place make them better than here."

Maddie hadn't even known he'd been to San Francisco before. But she was too famished to ask about it. Instead, she focused on savoring each bite, doing her best not to eat so fast that her bun disappeared before she was ready. However, even the most careful bites were too quick. Before she knew it, all she held was an empty bag, and her piqued appetite made her stomach rumble for more. It was the first real meal she'd had since they'd left New Mexico.

"So, who exactly are we staying with?" Maddie asked.

"It's my buddy Ben and his girlfriend. They live off Nineteenth Avenue on the other side of the city. They said we could stay there as long as we needed to." Maddie smiled at the news of the open invitation, forgetting in the moment that she had ever been disappointed about their temporary living arrangements. It would feel good to be settled instead of riding across country in a cramped car.

Jordan made a few more turns before slowing to a stop on a street of crowded homes. Each one was painted in vibrant colors of lime greens, baby blues, sherbet oranges, and brilliant pinks—like the one they were in front of now.

"This is it," he said, referring to the pink two-story home beside them. Maddie's eyes widened. It seemed so big, not at all what she had expected. Maybe this wouldn't be so bad.

There was no parking available on the street, and Jordan had to drive another block before he found an empty space. He pulled their things out of the car, and together they made the trek back down the hill to their new home.

Jordan led Maddie up the driveway and pressed the buzzer on the side of the gated door.

"Who is it?" a gruff voice asked through the speaker.

"It's Jordan, man."

"Oh, hey dude. Come on up. The door at the top of the stairs is unlocked." A buzzer sounded, and Jordan pulled the door open. A narrow passageway of stairs greeted them. Maddie pulled her bag up behind her, gripping the railing to keep herself from falling back by the weight of her belongings. She followed Jordan through the door at the top of the stairs.

"Yo! Jordan!" A guy with jet black hair and dark skin got up from the couch, and rushed over to clap Jordan on the back. Maddie looked around the apartment, surprised at how much smaller the house seemed once they were inside. There didn't seem to be any access to the first floor, and she realized it must have just been a garage or something. A quick survey of the second floor revealed a cramped living room, a kitchen off to the side, and several closed doors to what Maddie assumed were bedrooms and bathrooms. She wondered which room would be theirs.

"You must be the little mama," the guy from the couch said. He came over to her and gave her a hug. Strange scents mingled with his cologne against her face. She detected hints of weed, alcohol, and laundry detergent. He pulled away and gave her a grin. His teeth were crooked, and the scar over his eyebrow made his grey eyes appear menacing. But his smile was kind. Maddie couldn't help but give him a shy smile back.

"I'm Maddie," she told him.

"Hi Maddie, I'm Ben. My girlfriend, Julie, will be here later. She's just finishing up her shift at Chunky's." He nodded at the corner of the living room. "You can throw your stuff there for now. We have a couple other crashers here, too, so I hope you don't mind sharing the space."

"Of course not, dude. It's awesome of you to even let us stay," Jordan said. He handed Maddie his bag and jutted his chin toward the corner. Maddie hoped her disappointment wasn't apparent. It was obvious there was no bedroom for them—they would be sleeping in the living room. And by the looks of another pile of stuff in the room, the couch was already taken.

She set the bags down, arranging them as best as she could so they didn't take up too much space.

"You two will be sharing the living room with Abe and Jennifer," Ben continued. "They have this couch, which folds out into a bed. And you two can grab the spare mattress from the garage and sleep in the corner over there," he said, indicating the area where Maddie had just placed all their belongings. It was going to be tight quarters, but it would do.

Ben looked at his watch and whistled. "Dang," he said. "I didn't realize how late it was. You guys eat? I don't have much, just beer and peanut butter. I might even have a frozen pizza in the freezer."

"Nah, don't worry about it. We ate before we got here," Jordan said, squeezing Maddie's knee with intention. Maddie fumed inside, knowing it was his way to tell her to keep quiet. But she *was* hungry. The pork bun earlier had only made her appetite grow, and her stomach churned for more. She could feel tears of frustration, hunger, and exhaustion beginning to burn against her eyelids, but she willed them to stay at bay.

"Do you have a shower?" she blurted out, eager to just get out of the room and wash the last two days off of her. Ben showed her where it was, and Maddie took her bag of clothes into the room with her, hoping there was something clean among the miniscule amount of belongings she had left in the world.

The steam filled the bathroom, a cloud forming around the shower and leaving a glistening sheen on the walls and mirror. Maddie stood under the hot spray, inhaling the moist air. It seemed like forever since she had been able to take a decent shower, and she took a few moments to let the water engulf her, allowing it to pelt her back in tiny jabs. She didn't have any shampoo with her, so she used a small amount from the bottle on the shelf, helping herself to the conditioner next to it, as well. She moved on to the soap, smiling at the sweet fragrance before lathering up and rinsing off. When she was done, she dried off with the towel Ben had handed her, hanging it on the hook next to the other towels. After dressing, she found a comb in one of the drawers and ran it through her hair. She emerged from the room feeling rejuvenated and cozy. But the feeling dissipated when she saw Jordan on the couch, a few empty bottles of beer next to him, and a pan with one last slice of pizza between him and Ben. He started to reach for the slice, but paused when he saw Maddie.

"Well, don't you clean up nice," Jordan said. He lifted the pizza to his mouth.

"Is any of that for me?" Maddie asked, her eyes narrowing. Jordan caught her irritation and grinned, taking the slice away from his mouth and handing it over to her. Maddie stalked over to him and took it out of his hands, biting down into it, not even caring that they had an audience as she glared at him.

"Maddie, I was just teasing," Jordan said. She knew that was a lie. However, the pizza tasted so good, Maddie didn't want to take the time to argue with him. She polished it off in less than a minute, staring at the pan of crumbs as if she could manifest more where it came from.

"Are you going to get the mattress, or am I?" Maddie asked him. Both Jordan and Ben were slumped down on the couch. Maddie wondered if they'd only had beer, or if some other substance had made an appearance while she was gone.

"You can get it," Jordan said. Ben nudged him.

"Dude, she's pregnant," he hissed at Jordan. Ben turned to her. "We'll get it," he told her. The two of them stumbled out of the room and down the stairs while Maddie moved all of their belongings away from the corner. She was so exhausted, she didn't even care if they had a mattress of not. And she was so over the way Jordan was acting. She hoped that a good night's sleep might help everything go back to normal—whatever normal was now.

Jordan and Ben worked to get the mattress back up the stairs. Once they placed it in the corner, the two of them collapsed back on the couch.

"There are blankets in the closet over there," Ben said, waving his hand toward a closed door next to the bedroom. Maddie opened it and rummaged through the shelves of towels and random knickknacks that cluttered up the closet, finding some musty smelling sheets and a thin blanket to cover them. Then she set to making the bed, anxious to just crawl in and fall asleep. When she was done, she glanced back at Jordan. His head was back, a snore escaping his open mouth. Beside him, Ben winked at Maddie from the couch.

"Looks like he's out for the night," Ben chuckled. "You'll have to move him, though. This is where Jennifer and Abe are staying when they get back home." Then he retreated to his room.

"Babe, get up," Maddie whispered, shaking Jordan. He stirred, opening his eyes. Without saying a word, he stumbled to the bed Maddie had made on the floor, pulling the covers over him without even getting undressed. Maddie took the space next to him and tugged on the blanket until she had enough covering her. Despite a few lumps in the mattress, Maddie felt her body relax with relief.

She was almost asleep when she heard footsteps on the stairs, followed by the soft click of the door. Maddie kept her eyes closed to appear asleep, hearing as a woman gave a loud sigh. Maddie felt the woman walk past the mattress to Ben's bedroom, and wondered if this was Julie, Ben's girlfriend. She couldn't quite make out the conversation that followed behind the closed door, but a few words dropped like lead in her ears. *Freeloaders. Every stray person. Money. Job.* Maddie tuned out after a while. She couldn't help but empathize with this woman's anger, even as she bore the weight of guilt on her shoulders. She just hoped this woman would empathize as well, and not kick them out.

It took some time for Maddie's restless mind to quiet down, these new worries ping-ponging through her head every time she began to relax into sleep. She focused on Jordan's breathing, matching the rise and fall of his body with breaths of her own. Soon, Maddie's worries slipped out of her mind, replaced with a web of dreams she'd forget by morning.

- Eight -
Flipping Pancakes

Morning came too early. Jordan was still asleep when Maddie opened her eyes, squinting at the bright sunlight streaming through the window next to them. The couch was pulled out into a bed, and Maddie could see two sleeping bodies hidden under the blankets. She crept out from under the blanket, shivering at how much the room had cooled overnight. With cautious hands, she pulled the blinds down slow in an attempt to keep the room darker a little longer, and not wake anyone in the process. Then she darted back into bed and under the covers, scooting next to Jordan so she could use his body heat to warm up. He only stirred a little, but stayed asleep. Awake now, Maddie looked up at the couch bed, noticing a girl looking back at her. Her brown hair was cropped shorter than Maddie had ever seen on a girl. But it only seemed to make her features look that much more feminine, especially when she lifted her head to offer Maddie a small smile.

"Hi," the girl whispered.

"Hi," Maddie whispered back.

"Do you want some coffee?" she asked. Maddie shook her head no.

"I don't drink coffee," Maddie whispered. "But some tea would be nice." She pulled the covers back and followed the girl into the kitchen.

"I'm Jennifer," the girl said, taking two coffee cups out of the cupboard before starting the teakettle on the stove.

"I'm Maddie, and that's Jordan who's still asleep." She looked around the kitchen, wondering what she could do to help even as she didn't know where anything was. Jennifer waved her off. So Maddie sat at the table and watched the girl move through the kitchen, memorizing the contents of every cabinet and drawer Jennifer opened. *Cups in the upper right cabinet. Silverware in the second drawer to the right. Tea on the shelf near the window.* Jennifer moved through the kitchen in a long t-shirt just barely covering her tan legs, her bare feet silent as she danced across the linoleum. She placed a tea bag in a cup and poured hot water over it, then handed the steeping cup to Maddie.

"That's Abe on the couch," she said, pointing her hand toward the living room. "We were out late last night with friends, so I don't expect he'll wake up for a few hours. Do you take sugar?" Maddie nodded, and Jennifer hopped up and brought the sugar bowl back to her. "I don't," Jennifer continued. "I used to—a lot, actually. But one day I decided to drink it without sugar. It was gross at first, and then I just got used to it. Now I think it tastes nasty with sugar. You should try it sometime, drinking your tea without sugar. It's not that bad."

Maddie grinned at the girl's chatter, wondering how someone who drank coffee could be so awake before even taking a sip. As if reading her mind, Jennifer gave her a sheepish grin.

"Sorry, I'm talking too much. Abe is always on my case about it. I just get excited when I come across new friends. I'll stop, I promise."

"I don't mind," Maddie laughed. And she didn't. It was actually nice to have another girl around to chat with.

"No really, I'll stop. I want to hear about you, what brings you here, where you are from, how long you're staying, and what your plans are," Jennifer rattled off without coming up for air. She sat back, a look of expectation on her face as she waited for Maddie to appease her curiosity.

"Well, we just got in last night, obviously," Maddie started. "We drove all the way from New Mexico where we used to live. I guess Ben is an old buddy of Jordan's, although I don't know how. I've never met him, and I've been with Jordan for a year and a half."

"So, why did you leave? You're so young," Jennifer said.

"Well, when my parents found out I was pregnant—"

"You're pregnant?!" Jennifer exclaimed, her eyes shooting down to Maddie's belly. "I mean, of course you are. I can see your cute little belly. But I didn't realize..."

"You thought I was just fat?" Maddie asked, but she grinned to show she was joking.

"No, I actually didn't even notice at all until just now. How far along are you?"

"A little over three months, I think," Maddie said. "I managed to hide it from my parents for a while, but my belly just started expanding and they were bound to find out anyway. But when I told them, my parents kicked me out."

"That's so cruel!" Jennifer exclaimed. "If I had a daughter and she accidentally got pregnant, I'd probably help her out by raising the baby so she could get an education or whatever."

"Well, I didn't expect my parents to raise my baby," Maddie said. "But I just…" She paused, feeling her eyes well up with tears. It still stung that her dad had tossed her aside, treating her as if she were disposable just because she proved to not be his perfect little girl. What kind of parent did that? "All I know is that if my child comes home telling me she's in some kind of trouble, I'd be there to help her. I wouldn't make her leave because she messed up." Maddie looked away as she said it, swiping at the moisture in her eyes. She looked back at Jennifer and smiled. "Sorry, I hate to be a downer."

"You're not. It's real. And I get it. I'd have left, too. But aren't you scared? I mean, how old are you anyway?" Jennifer asked.

"I'm sixteen. And yeah, I'm terrified! I've never had a job, and I was supposed to be a junior in high school next year. Now I'll never graduate, and I don't know how we'll raise our kid on our own. I mean, Jordan can go get a job and all. But I don't know anything about San Francisco or California. I'm kind of relying on him to take care of us, and well…"

"It's hard to feel safe when you have to rely on someone else," Jennifer finished for her.

"Well, yeah," Maddie said. "I mean, kind of. It's hard when I've only had my parents taking care of me. Jordan might be eighteen and all, but he's not exactly a grownup. Can he take care of me? What about when the baby comes? His answer was to move us across the country to sleep on some stranger's floor." Just saying it out loud gave Maddie a sense of relief. It felt good to finally admit it outside of herself—that she didn't trust the situation, or that Jordan even knew what he was doing. Just remembering how quickly he'd changed when he was around Ben the night before made her question everything. In all the time they'd been together, she had never hung out with him around friends. It made her wonder if she really knew him at all.

"I'm sure everything will be all right," Jennifer encouraged her. "I mean, if he hadn't brought you here, we never would have met. And I can already tell we're going to be great friends."

Maddie smiled, but only briefly.

"I just don't know how long we're going to be allowed to stay," Maddie said, and then told Jennifer about the night before when Julie came home. "I don't think she's very happy we're here. By the tone of her voice, she didn't seem thrilled at all."

"Oh, don't mind Julie," Jennifer reassured her. "I can't say I blame her. Ben is always inviting people to stay here, and it's not even his place."

"It's not?" Maddie asked.

"Nope, it's Julie's. He's been out of work for as long as I can remember, and Julie let him move in with her. His way of repaying her is to keep moving people in while she's away at work. So I can't hold it against her when she gets irritated, especially since Abe and I are one of the pairs of couch surfers Ben has brought in. But at the same time, she's still with the guy even when it's obvious he's just using her for a place to crash. Who am I to judge, though? Maybe it's love," she said, shrugging her shoulders than sipping at her coffee. "Are you empty? Want any more?" Maddie nodded, and Jennifer took the cups to give them each a refill. "At any rate, Abe and I are moving out at the end of this week. It's time. We've been here three months, and are probably to blame for Julie's sour mood last night. We kind of overstayed our welcome. Besides, we found a cute little loft that's within our budget." Her eyes widened, and she grabbed Maddie's hand. "You should totally come over for dinner once we're all settled in!"

"Totally!" Maddie said back, matching Jennifer's enthusiasm. "And when the baby comes, you'll have to come see her."

"Oh! You know it's a girl?" Jennifer asked.

"Well, not exactly," Maddie admitted. "I mean, I haven't seen a doctor yet. But I just have this feeling she's a girl."

"You should really get a check-up. I mean, I don't want to get in your business and all. But it just seems like pregnant women go to the doctor's a lot."

"I know," Maddie said. "But all I have is my parent's insurance, and who knows if they've cancelled that or not.

Maybe when Jordan gets a job…" But even then, Maddie didn't know if that would be a solution. They weren't married. If Jordan got insurance through his job, would she be covered? Maddie wasn't sure what the answer to that was.

"Hey, I know where a free clinic is! It's just up the road a ways. I could take you there if you want." Maddie nodded her head yes, nervous all of a sudden. What if the doctor wouldn't see her until he'd met with her parents? What if it still cost money? "Great!" Jennifer exclaimed, unaware of Maddie's inner hesitation. "We'll go right after breakfast. I'm sure they'll be open."

Maddie got dressed in the bathroom, then folded all her belongings and placed them in the corner of the living room. The door to Ben and Julie's door opened, and a tall blonde-haired woman padded out in her pajamas and bare feet. She breezed past Maddie without saying a word to her. Jennifer glanced up from the kitchen table, then raised her eyebrow at Maddie across the apartment over the obvious brush off.

"Julie, have you met Maddie? She just drove in from New Mexico last night." She gave Julie a pointed look that said *play nice.'* Julie ignored the look and grabbed a cup from the cupboard to make herself a cup of coffee.

"I'm not really interested in meeting people who won't be sticking around very long," Julie said in a terse tone, turning her gaze to finally rest on Maddie. "They might take it as an invitation to stay longer."

"Julie, don't be like that. It's not her fault. Besides, she's pregnant," Jennifer pointed out, as if being pregnant meant people couldn't be mean to her.

"Oh, in that case, let's pull a crib out and put it in the living room. Better yet, they can have my bedroom," Julie stormed. She tilted her head back and laughed, though Maddie knew she wasn't really finding any humor in this. Julie's blatant remarks made Maddie fume on the inside. Regardless of who was in her house and whether she wanted them there or not, Maddie had done nothing to deserve this kind of treatment. She wanted to call Julie out on this, to tell her exactly where she could take that imaginary crib and shove it. But she also knew she needed a place to sleep that night, and she wasn't sure how many more nights would follow after that. She was at Julie's mercy, which made Julie the queen. If Julie was unfair to her about it, the only thing Maddie should do was smile and take it.

"I'm sorry," Maddie whispered, looking down at her feet. Julie sighed at the table.

"No, I'm sorry," she said. "I'm being mean. Let me start over. I'm Julie," and she stuck out her hand. Maddie walked over to the kitchen table and took her hand in a mutually feeble handshake. "There. Now we're friends," Julie said, even though Maddie could swear they were anything but.

"Let me make some pancakes for everyone," Jennifer announced, and went about the kitchen gathering ingredients. Maddie's stomach rumbled at the mention, reminding her of the miniscule dinner from the night before.

"Can I help?" she asked. Jennifer handed her a spatula and instructed her to flip the pancakes once the batter was done.

"Wait until you see bubbles forming before you turn them over," she told her once she'd ladled three perfect circles in the pan. Maddie kept a close eye on the pancakes. When it appeared there were bubbles, she went to turn one. It landed awkwardly on top of another pancake. She worked to separate them, but batter spread all over the spatula. She could hear Julie give a loud sigh behind her.

"Haven't you ever cooked before?" she asked Maddie, her tone dripping in exasperation. Maddie shook her head no. Her mom had always done that for her. "Move over," Julie commanded, getting up from the table.

"I'm just going to go take a shower," Jennifer announced, sneaking out of the room before anyone could protest. Maddie started to sit back down, but Julie made a noise. "I'm not doing it for you," she said. "I'm teaching you how it's done. You might as well learn something while you're here." She picked up the spatula and scraped the ruined pancakes into the garbage. Then she ladled three new circles of batter into the pan with a sizzle. She waited until large lumps breathed into the pancakes before slipping the spatula under one, lifting it up, and then dropping it back into the pan. She then did the same to the second one.

"The secret is to not be shy about flipping it," she instructed her. "You have to just act like you know what you're doing."

She gave Maddie the spatula to turn the last one. Maddie managed to get the utensil underneath the pancake, and only a small portion of it landed on another pancake. The majority of it landed correctly, sizzling in the pan. Maddie looked at Julie for approval. Julie kept her face stern, but Maddie caught a glimmer of acceptance in her eyes.

"Better," Julie said, going back to the table to sit.

Maddie continued cooking, ladling pancakes of various sizes into the pan and improving her flipping techniques with each turn. By the time she'd scraped the last of the batter from the bowl, she felt a bit more confident with the spatula. She added the last of the batch to a plate of pancakes warming in the oven, then moved the pans to the sink to begin washing them. Julie raised her eyes from the book she was reading, but she said nothing. When the dishes were all clean and the counters wiped down, Maddie grabbed a hot pad and placed the steaming pancakes on the table.

"Mmmm, just in time," Jennifer said, rubbing her short brown hair with the towel draped around her neck as she came into the kitchen. She grabbed the syrup from the cupboard while Maddie gathered a stack of plates and utensils. Then all three attacked the stack of pancakes at the table. They could hear stirring in the other room, signaling that the boys were starting to wake up.

"Maybe you all living here isn't such a bad thing," Julie said before diving into another bite. Despite the awkward and tense morning, even Maddie couldn't help but laugh with the other two.

Once the boys were up and Julie had left for work, Maddie and Jennifer took off in search of the free clinic. It was chilly and foggy outside despite the summer month, and Maddie wished she'd brought a better sweatshirt. She wrapped the thin one she was wearing around her.

"I thought this was California," she complained to Jennifer, who laughed in return.

"Are you expecting year-round bikini weather or something?" Jennifer asked. Maddie nodded, making Jennifer laugh even more. "That's only Southern California," Jennifer explained with a grin. "Up here we actually have seasons. And the Bay Area seasons are mostly year-round fog." Maddie wrinkled her nose in disappointment. "Don't worry," Jennifer said. "By afternoon, all of this will have burned off. Then we'll see some sun. But you'll want to take a sweatshirt wherever you go."

They reached the top of the hill, and Jennifer led Maddie down a side street where the clinic was. The hike up the steep sidewalk helped Maddie warm up some, allowing her to uncross her arms in front of her. But she still shivered with nervousness as they entered the building. They were greeted by a waiting room teeming with women and children, the sound of crying babies and yelling toddlers creating one static noise. Maddie immediately noticed that there weren't any men in the waiting room. Still, she couldn't help but wish she had brought Jordan in with her, just in case they got to hear the baby's heartbeat. She tried not to dwell too much on Jordan's disinterest back at the house when she had told him where they were going.

Jennifer led Maddie to the receptionist window. The woman behind the counter didn't pay them any attention, engrossed with the paperwork in front of her.

"Excuse me," Jennifer said. The woman still didn't look up. "My friend here is pregnant, and she'd like to see a doctor for a check-up."

"Have her add her name to the clipboard and her reason for being here. Then fill out this paperwork," the receptionist said, not even looking up as she slipped a clipboard through the slot in the window. "The doctor will be with you shortly." Maddie took the clipboard, then added her name to the list, adding "pregnant" as her ailment. She then followed Jennifer into the waiting room and filled out the paperwork as best as she could. When it came to address, however, she didn't know what to put.

"Just put Julie and Ben's address," Jennifer said, then recited the street address to her. Maddie felt funny about this, unsure how long she and Jordan would be staying there. Still, it was the closest place to home, for now.

The rest of the wait seemed to take forever. Maddie occupied herself by watching the children playing in the corner where a toy area was set up. Two boys fought over a box of blocks before one finally dumped the whole thing out. The other boy looked like he might throw a fit at the spilled blocks, but then thought better of it. He began building something out of the blocks closest to him. Just like that, the fight was over.

A few magazines lay on the table in front of them, and Maddie took the one that looked the most interesting. It was a few months old, and boasted of some celebrity gossip that Maddie knew had since been resolved. Still, it was more interesting than anything else in the room.

It was more than thirty minutes before Maddie's name was called. Jennifer stood, too. Maddie was suddenly really grateful she was here, knowing she didn't have to do this alone. The nurse led the two girls down a hallway and instructed Maddie to pee in a cup in the bathroom. After recording her weight, the nurse then showed the girls to a small room in the back. Maddie sat on the exam table while Jennifer took a chair next to her. It felt awkward to be in such tiny quarters, especially when Maddie was given instructions to undress and put on a gown. Jennifer grabbed a magazine and buried her nose in it, offering Maddie privacy while never leaving the room.

The wait for the doctor didn't take nearly as long as the wait in the waiting room. They heard a knock on the door before a short man with curly brown hair opened it and peeked in.

"Are you ready?" he asked. Maddie smiled and nodded, the butterflies doing acrobats in her stomach. "Hi," he said, extending his hand. "I'm Dr. Pierce. You must be Maddie." She nodded, shaking his hand, suddenly feeling shy. The doctor turned to Jennifer.

"And you're the….other mother?" Dr. Pierce asked. Jennifer threw her head back with a laugh.

"No," she giggled as Maddie hid her laugh behind a hand. "I'm just a friend."

"Well hi, just a friend," Dr. Pierce said.

"Jennifer," she said, still laughing. He nodded with a wink, then turned back to Maddie. He took her blood pressure while letting her know that everything was fine with her urine test.

"It did say you came down with a case of baby," he told her, which made Maddie laugh. The ice was broken as her hands rested on her belly.

Dr. Pierce pulled a machine forward and instructed her to lie down. Placing a blanket across her legs, he pulled her gown up enough to expose her stomach.

"This might be cold," he warned her before squirting some blue gel on her belly. He pulled a wand out and placed it in the gel, moving it around a little. Next to him, warped images appeared on the screen, moving around at the same speed of the wand until he paused and a shape began to make sense in Maddie's eyes.

"Is that her?" Maddie asked. "I mean, him or her? Is that the baby?"

"It sure is," the doctor said with a smile. He pointed out the baby's head, its beating heart, and where its hands and legs were. Beside her, Jennifer squealed with excitement over each body part, as if it were her baby, too. Maddie forgot all about her earlier nervousness as she leaned forward to watch the image on the screen. Her growing belly had just become more than a body part. Her baby was in there. Maddie studied her child on the screen, trying to see further than what she was being shown. She wanted to see who the baby looked like most, whether its eyes were brown like hers or blue like Jordan's, and how much hair was on its head. But none of that was apparent in the odd shapes on the black and white screen.

"Can you tell if it's a boy or a girl?" she asked.

"It looks like it's too soon," Dr. Pierce said as he studied the image on the screen. "You're about sixteen weeks pregnant right now. While sometimes we can tell that early, generally we wait until you're around eighteen weeks or later. We should be able to find out at your appointment next month."

Dr. Pierce supplied her with a bag of souvenirs to take home—some prenatal vitamins, a few pamphlets for reading, and an application for Medi-Cal.

"But I've only lived in California for one day," Maddie told him, the words feeling strange to say out loud.

"That shouldn't be a problem," Dr. Pierce said. He advised her to get the paperwork filled out as quickly as possible. "You're going to want to go to a hospital to have the baby," he explained. "Trust me, you won't want to be left with that kind of bill."

- Nine -
Not So Nice, After All

"I'm telling you, Maddie, there's nothing out there," Jordan said, lying on his back on the foldout couch in the dark living room. Jennifer and Abe had moved out two weeks before, leaving them the run of the living room and the sole title of couch surfers. It had been a month since they first showed up on Julie and Ben's doorstep, and Jordan still hadn't found work. Worse, the money was all gone.

"I don't understand," Maddie whispered, hoping they wouldn't wake Julie and Ben in the next room. "Where did $1,000 go in a month?"

"Did you think everything was free, Maddie?" he hissed. "Gas and food cost money. And without an income, it's not like that money was going to last forever."

"But…" she trailed off, deciding it was better not to argue. As far as she could tell, Julie was the one who bought all the food. Maddie hadn't seen a penny of that money, except for that one measly pork bun on their way into the city. But she knew pointing that out to Jordan wasn't going to solve anything—it would only end up in an argument.

"We can't stay here forever," Maddie said to him. "Julie's pissed we're still here. If we have nothing to give her to help out, we have no right to stay here."

"What am I supposed to do? I'm doing my best. I don't see you going out there every day looking for a job."

"Right. And I'm sure employers will be bending over backwards to hire a pregnant teenager with no job experience," Maddie snapped back at him.

"Well then give me a break. I've hit up every auto shop I pass by, and no one's hiring."

"Do you ask if they know of anything from other shops?" she asked him. He snorted in response.

"I think I know what I'm doing. I've looked for a job before, Maddie. Just leave me alone."

They both stayed silent. Maddie had to bite her tongue to keep from unleashing all the rage she was feeling inside. It wasn't that she minded living there. It was clean with a comfortable place to sleep at night. She liked the neighborhood, and the thought that she could walk to the ocean if she wanted to. She didn't even mind the fog so much. But what she did mind was that they were surviving on someone else's dime. She was losing faith in Jordan. Depending on Julie was like living with her parents again, except there was no love lost here. She couldn't help but think less of Jordan as he went out every day and came home with nothing. She couldn't even be sure he was looking for a job. She had her suspicions that he wasn't. How else could he explain how all that money was gone when they weren't paying for rent, food, or bills?

Jordan rolled over to her, placing his arm around her and pulling her towards him. Maddie pulled away, only to have him pull her in tighter.

"Jordan, not tonight," she said. Jordan moved his face into her hair, nuzzling against her ear and kissing her neck. "Come on, Jordan," she complained.

"Maddie, please," he whispered.

It was the last thing she wanted to do. She was still angry at him. But he continued to kiss at her neck, his hands wandering to the hem of her shirt and migrating over her belly. He touched it for a moment, his hand lingering over the expansion. He never touched her stomach. She noticed he never looked there, either. It was like he wanted to forget she was even pregnant. But the brief pause as his hand rested on her pregnant belly made her suck her breath in. His touch symbolized interest in their unborn child. Then his hand moved to her breast, and his mouth found hers. By then it was too late. She forgot she was angry, at least for the most part. But she brushed the remaining amount of resentment aside as she met his kiss, doing her best to move as slow as possible to keep the old springs of the couch from squeaking.

Jordan moved so he was on top of her, and he looked down into her face and smiled, the moonlight from the window illuminating his features.

"Still mad?" he asked.

"Yes," Maddie lied. "I'm furious."

"Anything I can do to help?" he asked, lifting her shirt up over her head. She lay underneath him in just her underwear, exposed to the whole room. The cool air on her skin made her break out in goosebumps, and she shivered.

"What if someone comes out," Maddie giggled in a whisper. Jordan leaned down and kissed her chest, migrating up to her neck, then catching her mouth in a long, drawn out promenade of lips and tongue.

"Let them watch," he whispered. In the moonlight, Maddie could catch the glint in his eye as he removed the rest of both of their clothing. Her anger at the situation, her disappointment in his failings, the fact that they were hundreds of miles away from home sleeping on someone else's couch at their mercy….all of it was forgotten as he made love to her on the foldout couch in the living room, both of them biting their lips to keep from waking up the rest of the house. When it was over, he stayed close to her, holding her tight to him as they fell asleep in each other's arms.

It felt like she had only been asleep for a few moments when Jordan woke her up. "We have to go," he whispered. He was already dressed, and was holding her clothes in his hands.

"Why? What's going on?" she asked.

"I'll explain later. Just get dressed and grab your things." Maddie put her clothes on and started to make the bed, but Jordan stopped her. "There's no time for that," he said.

"Jordan, we can't go yet. I have a doctor's appointment today." She was supposed to be there at nine, and she'd been anticipating it since she and Jennifer had set the date.

"You're not going," Jordan said. "Come on, we have to go," he urged her.

"But we were supposed to find out if the baby is a boy or girl," she whispered. He either didn't hear her, or he ignored her.

They crept out the door and down the stairs, then made their way up the street toward the car. Once in, Jordan pulled away from the curb and flipped a U-turn to head down the hill they had driven up. Maddie wanted to ask where they were going, but she bit back her curiosity. The clock on the dash said 5:27, the sky just beginning to lighten from a deep purple to a rosy pink. They crossed the Golden Gate Bridge for the first time since they'd reached California. Maddie looked up, trying to see the parts of the red towers that hid within the fog. To her right, she could see the city getting further and further away. A tunnel appeared in the distance, the entrance marked by a rainbow painted on it. They reached the colorful arc and drove under it and into the tunnel. Once on the other side, the city couldn't be seen.

"Where are we going?" she finally asked.

"Not sure yet," he said, fiddling with the radio. He found a rock station and turned the volume up, the music blaring through the small car and thumping at Maddie's heart. Jordan then reached into his pocket and pulled out a stack of cash, playing with it before putting it back. Maddie knew he did it for her benefit, to show off that he now had the money to take care of them both. She was afraid to ask how he got it, afraid of what he was going to say. They had just been desolate a few hours earlier. She didn't want to know the answer, sure that she already knew. But as much as she tried to refrain, the question bubbled over and escaped from her mouth.

"Did you steal from anyone in the house?"

He said nothing, which told her everything she was afraid of.

"Goddammit Jordan!" she spat out, scrunching down in her seat. She stared out the window, no longer sure she wanted to do this anymore. The desire to go back home was overwhelming. They drove in silence for another half hour before Jordan pulled off the highway. The sign said Petaluma, a town she'd never heard of before. Jordan parked in the lot of the closest open restaurant to grab a bite to eat. He hadn't said a word since displaying the money. But once their food was in front of them, he took the opportunity to speak.

"Look. We need to be able to make it, Maddie." His face held no hint of a smile as he spoke, his tone insinuating the border of anger.

"Who did the money come from, Jordan?" Maddie spat out.

"You know who it came from."

Maddie felt the tears coming, angry because of what Jordan said, and angrier that her natural reaction was to cry.

"They took us in, Jordan. You can't steal from someone who was already giving you everything," she hissed at him. She didn't want to cause a scene. The restaurant was near empty at the early hour. But still, she was afraid that someone would hear what was going on and arrest the two of them. More than that, she was ashamed. Julie already despised them for their constant need of handouts. For Jordan to steal from her? It was a new low. "I can't believe you took her money. She provided for us."

"Maddie, are you seriously this naïve?" he asked.

"What are you talking about?" she demanded.

"I'm talking about the fact that it's time you got off your high horse and understood things aren't always good or nice."

Maddie felt her blood boil.

"Nice? Are you kidding me? I've lived away from my parents' house for over a month. We've slept on the floor at some stranger's house. I'm pregnant and only sixteen years old. I've lost all my friends, everyone I know, and I'm not even sure where we're going to be tomorrow, or the next day, or the day after that. I hardly think things are all that good or nice."

"Yeah, but how are you eating, Maddie? Who made sure you had a warm place to sleep? Have you been doing all this? Has some white collar job been doing this? Could you even survive if I weren't here to do everything I can to make sure we're taken care of? No." He took another bite, chewing as she digested what he was saying to her. "Truth is, you wouldn't be so comfortable if it weren't for a little hustling on my part. So go ahead and stick your little nose up to anything that doesn't fit your idealistic view of America. But tell me this, how innocent are you when it's dirty money that's paying for that breakfast you're eating?"

The words tore at her when she realized he was right. She was no better than he was. The realization must have shone on her face, because he grinned at her, a glint in his eye.

"So, are you ready to start helping out, or what?"

Hours later, she was sitting in the back of a patrol car on her way to the police station. She hadn't wanted to steal the wallet, but Jordan had packaged the idea so neatly. It was time she helped out. If she couldn't do it with a normal job, she might as well try it his way. So the plan was set.

But now some lady was on her way to the hospital because of her, and Jordan had probably crossed state lines by now. She knew she'd never see him again, and she didn't know how she felt about that. She loved him, but not like she used to. It hurt that he could abandon her so easily, but it was also a relief to have the decision made for her. Still, she couldn't push away the fear swelling inside of her. Who would take care of her now?

The Crossroads

Jill

~ Ten ~
Mending the Broken

Jill was awake when Michael came to her bedside in the emergency room. She could hear the distinct sound of his footsteps, how his pants swished when he walked, and the way he breathed in deep when things bothered him. But she kept her eyes closed, hoping he would think she was asleep. She felt him sit next to her and take her good hand, and she did her best to remain as still as possible. She'd already gone through x-rays, revealing a nondisplaced break to her radius bone on her forearm. But it still hadn't been casted. For now, it lay in a sling across her chest, a steady IV stream of medication numbing the dull pain that still radiated through her body, starting with her arm.

Stroking her hand, Michael sighed again. Jill could hear the concern in his breath, or perhaps it was judgment. She couldn't even buy their groceries. She couldn't do anything right. She was a failure as a wife just like she was a failure as a mother. She knew he was thinking it. But when she peeked over at him, she was surprised to see his fallen face, and his cheeks wet with tears as he studied the floor.

Jill had only seen him cry twice in the past few months. The first was when she told him that Toby had died. He had met her at the hospital, and they sobbed in each other's arms before being able to face the doctor. The second was that night when they crawled into bed, the pain of their loss making sleep impossible. But after that, Michael was her rock. Even at the funeral, he took over at the microphone, reading the carefully prepared letter she wrote about Toby—a letter that proved too difficult to get through. He had taken it from her and read her words, sharing all ways their little boy had made the world a better place.

Sitting there next to him, Jill could see the way he was fighting the tears, even as they kept rolling down his cheeks. He still didn't know she was awake as he shuddered into his sorrow. She had been so focused on her loss that she had forgotten he was suffering, too. She recalled all the times he had mused over whether Toby would be into football or baseball, and how he had looked forward to him getting old enough for fishing or camping. There were so many things he had wanted to teach Toby, and all those plans were now laying in the ground with their son.

Jill shifted slightly, and Michael swiped at his reddened eyes, taking a deep breath before giving her a brave smile. She squeezed his hand that held hers, returning the smile.

"Are you okay?" she asked, causing him to chuckle in spite of his tears.

"I should be asking you that," he said.

"I'm okay," she said. "They have me all looped on drugs, so the pain's tolerable. So I'm all right. But are you?"

He opened his mouth, and she could almost see the protest about to come out. But then he stopped himself, taking another deep breath as his eyes filled with tears. Jill realized she'd never asked him that. He'd been so good about making sure she was okay by tending to her needs, as well as making sure she was taking care of herself. And never once had she returned the same level of care for him.

"Michael, I am so sorry," she whispered, her own eyes filling with tears.

"Honey, it wasn't your fault. You were just in the wrong place at the wrong time," he said.

"No, not that," Jill said. "I mean, I'm sorry I've been so self-focused. I have been so overwhelmed with my own pain over losing Toby that I kind of forgot that you were hurting, too." Michael opened his mouth to speak, but Jill stopped him. "Let me finish," she said. She could feel the tears starting to form in her eyes, but she willed them to stay at bay. For once, she needed to be the strong one. "I have no one to talk to about this. No one but you. There is nobody else who understands what it's like to lose a child, unless they've gone through it themselves. I'm so afraid to even bring it up to any of our friends who call the house, afraid that by doing so, I'm going to make them feel uncomfortable, or that they'll judge me for his death. And so I've just resorted to keeping silent about Toby, even to you. But I don't want to be silent anymore, Michael! Toby was alive! He was our son! He lived and breathed, he played, he laughed, he said words…he was a part of this world. I feel like by not talking about him, I'm pretending he doesn't even exist. And I'm afraid that I'll forget him."

"Sweetheart, you could never forget Toby," Michael said. He was no longer hiding his tears, letting them roll down his cheeks even as he smiled at her. In the moment, Jill felt like she had never loved him more. How could she have pushed him away? He was right there with her, missing Toby just as much as she was.

"It was my fault," she whispered.

"What do you mean?" he asked.

"I mean, I knew better. He never should have been standing in that cart. I knew that. If I had made him sit properly, he never would have fallen. And he'd be right here today."

Michael squeezed her good hand, moving closer so that his face was inches from hers.

"Do you think I blame you for Toby's death?" he asked. Jill whimpered, her face crinkling up. She nodded yes. "Honey, I don't blame you. I have never blamed you. It could have happened to anyone, at any time. It could have happened to me."

"But it didn't," Jill whispered. "It happened when he was with me."

"You know what I think?" he asked. He didn't wait for her answer. "I think we are all given a certain amount of time to fulfill whatever it is we're supposed to do before our time is up. Some of us are given a really long time. And some of us, like Toby, are able to do our life's work in a very short amount of time."

Jill used her blanket to mop at the tears in her eyes, but they were coming too fast. Michael moved to lean her head against him as carefully as he could without jarring her.

"Toby was a special little boy," he whispered into her hair, an unmistakable tear in his voice. "He was good and kind, he was smart and funny, and he was a joy to everyone who got to meet him. We were blessed to be his parents. We were given a really incredible gift to take care of while he was here. And even though we weren't ready yet, it was time to give him back." He let out the sob he was holding in, and she cried with him, her heart breaking and mending all at once.

"It's getting hard to remember what his laugh sounded like," Jill admitted in a whisper. "I mean, I don't always forget. Sometimes I think I hear him when I'm home alone. But there are times when I want to think about what he sounded like, and I can't. And when that girl stole my wallet, it wasn't the money I was worried about. It was Toby's pictures. If she took them, I might forget what he looked like in them." Jill motioned for her purse, and Michael grabbed it off the chair in the corner. She took the wallet out and opened it. Behind her driver's license, she pulled out three small photos and laid them on her lap. One was when Toby was just born, his tiny body held against her chest as she looked down at him. The second was just him, his olive eyes laughing into the camera above his dimpled, open-mouthed grin. The third was the most recent—Toby at Easter, holding a basket filled with colorful eggs. He was looking at her as she took the photo, pointing at the camera with a frustrated look on his face. She remembered at the time that he had wanted her to follow him, to stop taking photos and help him look for eggs. But she couldn't stop recording his every move, totally swept up in how he ran from egg to egg, wanting to memorize the amazement on his face every time he found one.

Michael picked the last one up and studied it, smiling even as his eyes remained rimmed with red.

"I think that little angry pout was my favorite look of his," Michael mused, wiping at his eyes. "I knew I wasn't supposed to laugh. But sometimes when he'd get so angry, it took all I had not to sweep him up and kiss that frustration off his face. He had the best pout ever."

A doctor stepped around the curtain that separated the beds in the emergency room, and both Jill and Michael looked up. Michael moved all the pictures off Jill's lap and slipped them back into the wallet. They both listened as the doctor re-explained the break in Jill's arm, holding the x-rays up to the light at the head of the bed. Then Michael followed as Jill was wheeled to another room to be casted. An hour later, and Jill was sporting a large white cast and getting ready to leave the hospital. But a police officer stopped them before they could go.

"Mrs. Johnson, can I have a few moments of your time before you leave," the officer asked.

"Is this really necessary right now?" Michael asked, stepping in. "My wife has had a long day, and we'd just like to go home."

"I understand that, Mr. Johnson," the officer said. "But we'll need a statement from your wife eventually. It's better to do it now while the details are still fresh than later when things might be forgotten."

"But I don't want to press charges against that girl— Maddie, I think that was her name. I don't want to press charges against Maddie." Both the officer and Michael looked at Jill.

"You don't?" Michael asked, disbelief on his face. "Honey, that girl almost took off with your wallet. She would have had access to all our credit cards, all your money, and our address." He paused, searching her face. "Jill, she would have taken those photos of Toby."

"But she didn't," Jill said.

"But she could have," Michael repeated. Jill sighed, looking from her husband to the officer.

"Sir, I don't want to press charges," she said again. "I have all my things, and no harm was done."

"No harm?" Michael exploded. "That girl broke your arm!"

"No, I broke my arm," Jill said. "We were both falling, and I was afraid the baby was going to get hurt. She was pregnant, Michael. If I didn't grab her, she would have fallen on the baby."

"Well that just takes the cake," Michael muttered. "She's pregnant and stealing other people's money. What a great example she's going to be for that child of hers."

"She was desperate!" Jill exclaimed. "I could see it in her eyes. She was desperate, and so young. I don't even think she has a home. The guy she was with took off, and by the way she screamed after him, I don't think he's coming back. Michael, I don't want something like this to go on her record. I don't want to be the one to put it there."

"But it's not your fault it would go on her record, it's her's," Michael said. "And besides, if she gets away with this, who's to say she won't do this to someone else?"

"I don't care," Jill said. "I don't want to press charges."

"Well, ma'am, with all due respect, the store owner is still within his right to press charges," the officer said.

"Why? She didn't steal anything from him," Jill said, her resolve standing firm.

"So you're saying she just stole from you."

"I'm not saying anything," she replied.

"Excuse me?"

"I said no," she repeated. "It's my right. You can get all the details from the store, if you need them. But not from me. I don't want to be a part of your investigation on Maddie."

The officer stared at her for a moment, appearing to wait for her to change her mind. But Jill refused to budge. The officer closed his notebook and put it back inside his vest.

"If you change your mind, come on down to the station," he said. Then he turned and walked out of the hospital.

"I don't understand you sometimes, Jill," Michael said when the officer was gone.

"You weren't there, Michael. You didn't see the look on her face. She couldn't have been older than sixteen."

"That doesn't matter!" Michael said. "It doesn't excuse the fact that she is stealing other people's money to get by."

"What if she has no other way? What if that's the only way she was going to be able to eat today?"

"What if she was going to use that money to buy drugs, Jill? Ever thought of that?"

"She wasn't," Jill muttered.

"How can you know that?"

"I can't!" Jill yelled. "But I just know! That girl was in trouble. It doesn't make stealing right, but sometimes you do crazy things when you're backed into a corner. And she was pregnant!"

"Is that what this is all about?" Michael asked.

"What do you mean?"

"I mean, that girl is about to have a baby. You just lost your baby. Could your judgment be clouded because of that?"

"No," she said, then looked at her hands. "I mean, maybe. I don't know." She looked up at him, wincing. "It doesn't matter though. My decision is final. I'm not pressing charges against that girl. I can't."

Michael sighed, and Jill could see his resolve softening. He looked at her, the frustration in his eyes evaporating. Finally, he smiled and gave a small laugh.

"This is why I love you, you know," he said. "You have the kindest heart. It's frustrating at times. But it's also endearing."

"I'm not always kind," Jill said, thinking of the past few selfish months. "But I try. It's the least I can do. Now, can we just go home? I'm ready to put this day behind us and start moving forward."

Maddie

~ Eleven ~
Taking Out the Garbage

The officer had driven Maddie to a juvenile detention center, sitting her down at a desk beyond a huge metal door so he could ask her question after question, sometimes the same question several times over. She tried to keep her face stoic, acting as if this was no big deal. But inside she was terrified. What was going to happen to her? Were they going to take her to jail? Would she stay here at the center? If they let her go, where would she go from there? How was she going to live?

When the questioning was over, she was sent to a holding cell to wait. She had tuned out during some of the questioning, which, at times, had felt more like lecturing. *Why would you steal the wallet? Who told you to do it? Who else was involved in the incident?* She couldn't help but let her mind wander, answering "yes" and "no" at what she hoped were the appropriate times. She heard mention of an emergency foster home, which sounded much more inviting than sitting in a holding cell. She also heard mention of her parents, which both terrified her and made her hopeful. It wasn't about whether they would be mad. There was no doubt her dad would be furious. What scared her more was if they didn't even care enough to come get her, if the option presented itself. But in line with that fear was the hope they would bring her home. She was done with running. She'd live by their rules. Maybe if they saw her larger belly, the evidence that she was pregnant while out on her own, they'd welcome her home and the arrival of their grandchild. At the very least, maybe they'd learn to accept the mere existence of him or her.

Maddie spent the night in the center, sleeping on a thin mattress over hard springs in a room with three other girls. Maddie ignored them all, and was relieved when they didn't pay her any attention at all. The bed was less comfortable then the foldout couch at Ben and Julie's, and the sound of metal doors banging kept waking her up. But she recognized this might be her last for sure deal, that for now she had a roof over her head and a meal coming in the morning. She knew that she should embrace it while she could.

Her parents showed up the next day. Maddie walked down the hall of the center, followed by a female officer. Once facing her parents, Maddie noticed the redness in her mother's eyes, as if she had been crying for days. Her mom let out a sob as soon as their eyes met. Maddie could hardly look her dad in the eye, but she stole a glance when she thought it was safe. He looked tired, his hardened expression softened at the edges by hints of aging. It had only been a month, but both of her parents felt like strangers. They also felt like home.

"Have you eaten?" her mother asked. Maddie nodded yes, though the pale egg and dry toast they had served for breakfast wasn't sticking to her. It was nearing noon, and Maddie could feel her stomach threatening to rumble. "Well, are you hungry?" Thank goodness for her mother's need to nurture, particularly with food. Maddie nodded yes again, offering her mom a small smile. Her mother returned it, taking her hand. "It's good to see you." She said it as if they hadn't kicked her out—as if they had just been separated for a short time and were now coming together for a pleasant visit. Maddie squeezed her mom's hand tight, grateful for the warmth in her touch, hoping the past could be forgiven and she could come home.

"Come on, Carol, let's go," her father's gruff voice interrupted. He pushed past them and out of the facility. Maddie and her mother followed close behind, getting in the car.

Maddie felt a lump in her throat when they pulled into the parking lot of a nearby restaurant. Just across the way was the exact store she had been at a day earlier—a day she wanted to forget. It wasn't like her to steal. It went against everything she believed. But when Jordan pointed out that she was no better than him for using that stolen money, it somehow manipulated her morals. Still, she knew better. And now she was paying the price for Jordan's mistakes. No, not just Jordan's—her mistakes, too.

Her father led the family to a table by the window where Maddie had a full view of the grocery store from where she sat. She could almost see the taillights of Jordan's car as he pulled out of the parking lot. She turned her head away, trying to ignore the sick feeling that weighed like a brick in her belly. Maybe it was supposed to happen this way. Maybe this whole nightmare was just the catalyst for reuniting her with her parents.

The waitress handed each of them a menu, and Maddie buried her nose in it to avoid having to answer any questions they might have for her. However, even when the food was ordered, no questions arose. Instead, an awkward silence hung over the table, creating a barrier between what they should say, and what they really wanted to say. Maddie's mother finally broke the ice.

"I've never been to California," she said. "I always wanted to go, but never found a way to get here." She offered Maddie an embarrassed smile, all of them aware these were hardly the ideal conditions for an excursion. Maddie's dad stayed silent, sipping his water while looking at anything and everything but Maddie.

"Neither have I," Maddie said, and then gave a nervous laugh when she realized how stupid that sounded. "I mean, it's kind of been nice living here for a short time. I mean…" She trailed off, having a hard time knowing what to say. Everything seemed so strange—her parents, the restaurant, being away from Jordan, being the kid again… "I really miss home," she blurted out, laying all niceties aside. "And I really miss you." Her mother smiled, taking Maddie's hand as her eyes filled with tears.

"I missed you, too," she said, then looked at her husband. "We both miss you," she corrected herself. "The house just isn't the same without you."

Maddie's dad kept his eyes focused on something unseen outside the window, the expression on his face unchanging as he chewed one bite after another.

"Has it been hard?" her mother asked. Maddie went into a light synopsis of the past few weeks, leaving a few bits and pieces out, and stopping just before she found herself in a grocery store, stealing some stranger's wallet. Her dad finally dropped his fork on his plate and turned to face Maddie.

"And how did you end up under arrest, Maddie?" he asked her. Maddie gave him a pained look as she squirmed in her seat.

"Bill, please," her mother pleaded with him, her hand resting on his arm. He brushed her off.

"No Carol, I want her to explain. Tell us Maddie, why did we have to pick our pregnant teenage daughter up from a detention center all the way in Petaluma, California?" He sat back and rested his folded arms on the table in front of him as he waited for her answer.

"Because I tried to steal someone's wallet," Maddie said in a small voice. She kept her eyes trained on the table, feeling his glare reach straight through her.

"You see, Carol?" her father said, turning to his wife. "You're so ready to pretend like everything is okay and will be so normal when we go home. But she's a dirty thief. Who's to say she won't try and steal from you or me when we take her home?"

"It's not like that, Dad!" Maddie said, raising her voice. She could feel the people around her turning their eyes toward them, but she was too enraged to care. "We had no money. We had no jobs. No one is going to hire a teenage girl, especially one that's pregnant! We had to eat somehow. We needed money to be able to find a place to sleep, or to at least have gas for our car!"

"Jordan should have been providing for you. At the very least, you should have stayed in his parent's house. He had a job there. Why the hell did you guys leave with nowhere to go to?" he demanded.

"Because his father…" She bit her lip to keep the words from falling out of her mouth. She wanted to tell them everything—how Jordan's father had attacked her, and what would have happened if Jordan hadn't walked in and saved her. She wanted to shove it in his face that they had thrown her to the wolves just because she was pregnant. She wanted to haunt them both with their decision, to describe what it was like living in that house, to give them every detail of the attack—from the putrid smell of Stan's tobacco breath to the way the alcohol stunk on his skin. But she couldn't. They wouldn't understand. Her father probably wouldn't even care.

"Because his father didn't want us there anymore," she lied, hanging her head.

"You sure know how to pick them," he shot at her.

Maddie burned at this, her eyes narrowing. Her own father had been the first to kick her out. His judgment over her version of what happened was insulting to her.

"The problem is, Maddie, you just don't think," her father continued. "You got pregnant by a boy who can't support you. You two took off without a plan to a place neither of you are familiar with. And instead of finding a respectable way to support yourselves, you've resorted to petty theft. We did not raise you this way."

"No! You raised me to be a good girl who always did what she was told, a girl who was not allowed to have a mind of her own!" she shouted at him, unable to hold back any longer. "You taught me to please others instead of thinking about what's best for myself. You taught me that I'm loved if I get good grades and behave myself, but I'll be hated if I step out of line. You taught me that to be noticed, I have to go to some pretty drastic measures. You taught me that everything needs to fit into its own neat little package, and if it doesn't fit, it's best just to discard it like a piece of trash—even if it's your own daughter!" She yelled the last sentence, slamming her hand on the table as she got up. Her belly hit the table as she tried to stand, and she put her hand over it out of instinct. Both her parents looked at her stomach as if they'd forgotten she was pregnant. Her dad was the first to look away.

Maddie rushed from the table, passing by people at the other tables who were whispering with furtive glances in her direction. She ignored them and ran into the bathroom, locking herself in a stall before releasing the sob that had been building inside. For five full minutes, her heart broke all over the dirty bathroom floor. She cried about Jordan leaving her, and abandoning their child in the process. She cried about the woman whose arm she may or may not have broken. She cried about having to grow up faster than she was ready to, missing the innocence she took for granted before all this mess started. She cried about her bedroom at home, her safe place where she could retreat to when life felt too hard or unfair. And she cried about missing her parents—the ones who loved her and protected her in a childhood that seemed so long ago. They weren't the people at the table. The parents she loved would have supported her upon finding out she was pregnant, held her hand the whole way through, and loved her and her child because they were family. The parents she loved would never have forced her to leave her childhood home and live on the streets.

Maddie wiped her eyes and left the stall, pausing in front of the mirror. She hadn't slept well since waking up early the day before, but the tiredness was hidden behind the puffy redness of her eyes. Her dark hair was a tangled mess, having not been brushed in days, and her bare face was pale underneath the red blotches from crying. It made her appear younger than her sixteen years. She was wearing the same clothes she put on two days ago, the same ratty clothes she wore often since she didn't have much to choose from. Now, she had even fewer. The small amount of items she had left were in Jordan's car, wherever he was, and if he even bothered to keep them. Maddie had a suspicion he threw them out the first chance he got, finally free from the pregnant anchor weighing him down.

Turning the faucet on, Maddie rinsed her face with cool water. The sensation of cold on her hot skin woke her up from the fog she had been under. She held her breath, throwing more and more water on her face until her lungs felt like bursting. Then she dried her face and hands and looked back in the mirror. Her eyes appeared less red against the flush in her cheeks, and the urge to cry had passed. She needed to put this all behind her. She needed to ask for her parents' forgiveness. She needed them to take her home.

The table at the front of the restaurant was empty when Maddie emerged from the bathroom. The bill was placed at the edge, and the waitress picked it up as she passed by. She looked up as Maddie approached and smiled.

"Did you see where they went?" Maddie asked, masking her fear.

"Right out there," the waitress said, pointing out the window. Maddie saw her parents rushing to the rental car, her father's hand firmly on her mother's elbow as he pulled her along. Her mom kept looking back, clearly arguing with her dad as he forced her to keep moving. Maddie realized what was going on and sprinted out the restaurant door.

"Stop!" she screamed, racing after them. They were already in the car, the brake lights red as her dad gunned the motor. "Wait! Please! Don't leave me here! Please! I have nowhere to go!" she pleaded. Her mother's window was down, and Maddie could see her leaning out the window while they backed up. "Mom!" Maddie screamed. The look on her mother's face said it all. There was no stopping them. Her mother, as much as she loved her daughter, loved Maddie's father more. And her dad was not going to support a daughter who did nothing but disappoint them.

She was being thrown away like a piece of trash.

Maddie stopped running and watched as her parents' car moved toward the edge of the parking lot, disappearing into traffic as they turned right and headed for the freeway.

She sat on the edge of the curb and placed her head on her knees, covering her arms over her to protect herself from the pain. In the last couple of weeks, she hadn't known what the next day would bring, each day more unpredictable than the last. But this time it was different—she had no one to rely on but herself. She had no money. She had no place to sleep. The meal she had just eaten with her parents was possibly the last one she'd get for a while. If she didn't figure something out, she was done for.

"Are you okay?" the waitress asked, sitting next to her on the curb. Maddie looked up and wiped her eyes. "I'm sorry, I saw the whole thing. Were they your parents?" she asked. Maddie paused. But then she nodded yes. "It will all be okay," the waitress said, offering Maddie a hopeful smile. "Sometimes I get in fights with my parents, too. They might just need a bit of a cooling off period or something. Give them some time before you head home, okay?" She squeezed Maddie's arm, still smiling at her. Maddie smiled back and nodded. She didn't have the heart to tell the woman that her home was all the way in New Mexico, and that she'd probably never see her parents again.

Jill

- Twelve -
Learning to Breathe

"How are you? Did you sleep okay?" Michael asked Jill as he came into their bedroom with a cup of coffee for each of them. He placed hers on the coaster she kept atop her dresser, then sat gingerly next to her on the bed holding his.

"I'm okay," she said. "I'm a little sore, but I slept okay." She moved to sit up and winced. She was more than a little sore. Her left arm throbbed underneath the cast, and every muscle in her body ached as if she'd been beat up rather than bruised from the fall. She stretched her good arm over her broken one to get the coffee, but was unable to get a good grip with just one hand since her dresser was on her left side.

"Sorry, let me help you," Michael said. He reached over and picked her coffee up, then placed it in her hand. Jill gave him a small smile. But inside she was growing frustrated about how difficult simple tasks would be for the next few weeks. But her dark mood evaporated with the first sip.

"Mmm, thank you for the coffee. This is perfect." She took a few more sips and then handed it back to him so he could put it on the dresser. "Just stay right there until I want another sip, okay?" she teased. He laughed and leaned over to kiss her forehead. The fresh smell of his just-washed hair and clean-shaven face made her pause, and she looked at him. She hadn't even heard him get in the shower. Now he stood before her wearing a button-down shirt with shorts, appearing ready to walk out the door even though he'd promised to stay home with her. "Are you going somewhere?" she asked.

"Just to the grocery store," he said. She ducked her head, remembering all the groceries that were left at the store in her failed attempt to shop. Her mood shift wasn't lost on him. "Hey, don't worry about it, okay? I actually don't mind shopping. I'm just going to grab a few things and then head home. I shouldn't be gone long, okay?"

"If you could wait a few minutes, I could be dressed and ready to go," Jill said, flipping the covers off her and preparing to stand. She fought against her body aches, concealing how much it hurt.

"No, you should rest. You've had a really eventful day. I'll only be gone a half hour tops, anyway," he said.

Jill wasn't fooled. She knew what he was doing. He was protecting her from herself. He didn't want her to face the grocery store at all when so much trauma surrounded it. But what he didn't know was that the near-robbery had awoken something inside her. She felt alive, possibly for the first time since losing Toby. She hadn't remembered the last time she felt adrenaline pumping through her veins, or feeling anything more intense than a somber state of grief. Even a fractured arm proved to be an exhilarating experience. Feeling pain on the outside of her body consumed the immeasurable mental pain she'd been living with for months. Jill realized she was ready to live again—not necessarily to move on, but to learn how to live in this new reality where Toby didn't exist.

"I want to go with you," Jill insisted. She stood, wincing before she could stop herself as the tenderness in her legs and back caught up with the dull ache in her arm.

"Jill, you can barely move without hurting. You've been through a lot. Just take it easy today and let me take care of everything." Michael held a concerned look in his eyes, but Jill just shook her head and moved to the closet to find something to wear that was easy to slip over her casted arm.

"I've spent the last three months as a prisoner of my sadness, Michael. Since Toby died, I haven't seen much more than the walls inside this house. I'm restless. I can't live like this anymore. If I have to take it easy one more day by avoiding the outside world, I'm either going to slip into hermithood, or just go insane." She pulled a casual sundress from the closet and held it up to her. Deciding it would work, she turned to her husband and gave him a soft smile. "Look, I'm not offering to do all the grocery shopping today. But I would like to spend some time with you." It occurred to her how much she had missed him. He'd been there the whole time, but it felt like years since she had actually *seen* him. She laid the dress on the bed and took his hand with her good one, squeezing it. He smiled at her and clasped his fingers with hers, looking at their hands intertwined.

"I'd love for you to come with me," he relented. "Maybe we could grab a bite to eat before shopping," he said. "But are you sure it won't be too much? Your body went through a lot yesterday."

"I'm fine," she insisted. "Just sore. Moving around will do me good, probably even work out the kinks. Now help me get dressed."

They arrived at their favorite café overlooking the Petaluma River, taking a table near the window to avoid the summer heat outside. The waitress brought them each bagels topped with smoked salmon, a small bowl of capers sitting next to Jill's on the plate. As they ate, Jill couldn't help but notice how different it was without a toddler in tow. She didn't know what to say or do, so accustomed to taking care of Toby's needs before being able to get her first bite. She and Michael ate their first few mouthfuls in silence, offering shy glances at each other before looking away. Jill could tell Michael was sensing the same awkwardness.

"Strange, isn't it?" she said. He gave a soft laugh, a sad smile on his face.

"Yeah. I keep waiting for him to pipe up or throw something," he said. And just like that, the conversation opened up. They talked about Toby a little more, but it migrated into talk of everyday life, which eventually turned into talk about Michael's job. As he shared about the triumphs and tribulations of his career, Jill's mind began to wander about her own future possibilities. What if….

"What if I got a job?" she mused. She looked up just in time to catch the relieved expression on Michael's face. "What?" she asked. He gave an embarrassed laugh.

"Sorry," he said. "I didn't mean to make that so obvious. It's just that…"

"I've been kind of a lump lately?" she guessed.

"No! That's not what I mean at all. It's more like, getting out of the house will do you some good. You devoted so much of yourself to being Toby's mom that when he…" Michael trailed off, pausing at the word they both knew ended the sentence. "I haven't wanted to press you before you were ready," he finished. "But I also know that without Toby, all you've had to focus on was loss."

Jill nodded in agreement. It made getting a job that much more important. She couldn't lay on the couch any longer. If she did, she was bound to disappear inside her grief. And the thought of being home alone, haunted by Toby's cries within her head… She needed to find something, anything that would save her from herself.

"I'm not even sure what I'll do," she said to Michael. "It's been so long since I've worked, and it's not like I had some lucrative career before Toby was born." Her voice wobbled a little as she said his name. She had tried not to think about it—what moving beyond Toby would feel like. When he'd first died, she could think of nothing else. And now here she was, planning a life without him. "Am I a bad mom?" she asked, then realized again what she'd said. A mom. Was she even a mom anymore? "I mean, am I bad person?" she corrected herself.

"You are not a bad person, or a bad mom. Why would you even ask?"

"Because it's only been three months, and here I am, moving on like Toby didn't even matter." As soon as the words came out of her mouth, she burst into tears, surprising the both of them. "Sorry," she whimpered. "I don't mean to… I mean…" Michael moved from his side of the booth and slid onto her side, putting his arm around her and pulling her head against his chest. She shuddered, burying her face against his shirt. She didn't want to cry. She was done with crying. But how could she move beyond this hurt?

"Jill, you are a wonderful person, and a wonderful mother. Continuing to live life would be an honor to Toby's memory. Do you think Toby would have wanted you to be stuck in limbo for the rest of your life?"

"No," Jill whispered. "But it doesn't make me feel any less horrible for even thinking of moving forward."

"I went back to work," Michael pointed out. "Does that mean I love Toby less?"

"Of course not," Jill said, then felt the weight of guilt lift off her shoulders as she realized his point. She moved her head away from his chest and gave him a tear-stained smile. "Thank you," she said.

Michael paid the bill, and they drove to the grocery store. Jill redirected him once she realized he was heading toward the store near their house, pointing him to the store she'd been at the day before instead.

"Are you sure?" Michael asked. "I mean, some girl tried to rob you there. We don't need to shop at a place like that."

"I know. But I can't go back to Hal's Market. Not now, maybe not ever," she told him.

"Well, there are other stores," he said. "We could go to that market up on Keller Street, or the one on the other side of town."

"Let's just go here. It's right there, anyway," she said, pointing a few yards ahead. Michael put on his blinker and slowed to turn left. But just as he entered, they were almost sideswiped by a car making a sharp right turn out of the lot.

"Whoa," Michael breathed, jerking the steering wheel to the right to avoid getting hit. Jill only caught a glance of the people in the car, noticing they were arguing over something. It explained the driver's failure to pay attention to any cars around him.

"That guy had better start focusing on his driving or he's going to kill someone," Jill mused. As they pulled forward, she noticed a girl sitting on the edge of the sidewalk with her head resting on her knees. A waitress came out of the restaurant behind her and put her arm around the crying girl. Michael drove by them too fast for Jill to see much more than that, but it struck her how odd it all seemed. Between the arguing couple and this crying girl, it seemed the whole world was absorbing the pain she was trying to let go of.

Michael found a parking spot and they both walked to the store. Jill was prepared this time with a quarter, and she placed it in the slot. Michael gave her an amused look.

"So this is where you've been shopping, huh?" he chuckled, eying the quarter in the slot as they rolled the cart into the shop.

"Hey, it might not be fancy, but the prices are great," Jill laughed. "Or so I've heard. I've never actually bought anything here yet." She smirked, and then added, "Make sure you check the expiration dates, though."

They perused the aisles together almost as if the experience was just a part of their impromptu morning date. Michael pushed the cart while Jill walked beside him. Her muscles weren't quite as sore as they'd felt that morning, though her arm was starting to throb inside the sling at her chest. She was due for another pain pill, but that would have to wait until she got home since the bottle was sitting on her dresser in their bedroom. For now, she traveled the maze of aisles with Michael at a slow speed, following the train of families with squirming children before finding the last item on their list and heading to the checkout stand. As they exited the parking lot, Jill scanned the sidewalk for the crying girl, wondering if it would be weird to Michael if they stopped so she could see if there was anything she could do to help. But the sidewalk curb was empty when they drove by, the girl nowhere to be found.

"Everything okay?" Michael asked as Jill craned her neck to look around the lot. She stopped looking and gave him a smile.

"Everything's fine," she said. Everything wasn't fine. Not without Toby. But it was on its way to being bearable. That was better than anything she had felt in the past three months.

Jill

~ Thirteen ~
A Clean Slate

Jill stood outside the doorway of Toby's room, her hand on the doorknob. She had told Michael before he left that morning that she would be spending the day looking for work. But she also knew that before she could think of moving forward with a job, she had other work to do—and it had everything to do with Toby's room.

In her mind, she could see every nook and cranny of the room, remembering each time she sat in the rocking chair to soothe him to sleep or sat cross-legged on the floor playing trucks with him. She knew each one of his toys he played with, which ones were his favorites, and which ones lay untouched at the bottom of the toy box. She knew the crib he slept in, the mobiles she hung out of his reach on the ceiling, and his green walls with the happy yellow giraffes she had painted when he was just a sweet little nugget in her belly.

But she hadn't been in there since the day she found him unresponsive in his crib. After Michael had cleaned the room, the door remained closed for good.

Jill took a few deep breaths and let them out slow. She needed to do this. Even if she only opened the door and looked in, it was enough to call it a success in her goal to keep moving forward. But what she really wanted to do was bigger than that. She needed to bag his things up and get them out of the house. She didn't want to erase Toby from their home. But she needed to do something so that he wasn't stuck in this portion of the house, haunting her with the mere presence of his things.

With a shaky hand, Jill eased the door open. The blinds were shut, casting a dark shadow over the room. The closed windows made the air in the room smell musty. She let out another slow breath, gathering up the courage to cross the threshold and enter the room.

"Just do it already," she whispered. She entered the room, passing by the crib to reach the window and open the blinds. Sunlight streamed in through the blinds, illuminating the starkness of the clean room, every item in its place as if it were a showroom. She lifted the blinds and opened the windows, inviting the sound of chirping birds inside the somber remnants of the space around her. Only then did she turn around and survey her surroundings.

Everything was just as she remembered, just cleaner. The toys were all hidden within the toy box. When she opened the box, she was relieved to see that Michael had even cleaned up where she had gotten sick. The floor was vacuumed, still possessing the lines in the light brown carpet as if it had just been groomed. And in the middle of the room was the crib. Jill walked over to it, running her hand over the wooden railing as she thought of all the times she'd peered over to watch as Toby slept. The mattress was now bare, the pale green of the glossy mattress now staring back up at her. For a moment, the image of Toby's sleeping body was replaced by the vision of when she last saw him, the ashen color of his skin next to the vomit on his mattress. Jill felt her knees grow weak, and she held on to the crib for support, fighting at the tears that threatened to drive her back to the couch and away from the room.

"No," she said out loud to the room, looking around her at the happy green walls and yellow giraffes. She forced that last image out, replacing it with thoughts of Toby running down the hall, playing hide-and-seek through the rooms, and hurtling himself into her arms whenever she found him. She smiled, the tears still managing to break through, coursing down her cheeks. This was how she always wanted to remember him—for the lovable, playful boy he was.

Jill went to his clothing drawer first, pulling the drawers open and then taking each article out one by one. She made piles in the room—one for saving as keepsakes, and the other to give away. At first, the keepsake pile grew while the donation pile remained bare. But soon, she found it in herself to start adding to the donation pile, knowing that anything she kept would only serve as a step toward sadness.

When the drawers were empty, she went to the toys. She saved all of his favorite ones, placing them in a box she reserved for the attic. The rest, she piled with the clothes. When it was done, she gathered everything up and put them in plastic garbage bags. She tried to lift one of the bags, but realized how limited she was with just one good arm. So instead she just dragged each bag out to the hallway, lining them against the wall to create a pathway.

The crib was the hardest. But she knew she couldn't keep it. As many happy memories were associated with it, the very last memory tainted it. With a screwdriver in her good hand and some tricky balancing with her casted arm, she began dismantling it. Soon, it lay in pieces in the middle of the room. Unsure what to do with it, Jill left it there and took another look around the room. All that was left were the walls. She had considered leaving them the way they were. But everything she had accomplished so far only built up her momentum to continue until she was done. She knew that if she stopped, that would be the end; she'd never begin again. So she went out to the garage and got the leftover paint from when she painted the living room, and carried it into the back room. She laid drop cloths down around the edges of the room, and managed to tape off the baseboard with her good arm. Her casted arm ached, and she could feel the rest of her body following suit. The sun was beginning to dim, and she turned on the light to illuminate the walls. With some difficulty, she poured a good amount of paint into the roller pan. She fought through her exhaustion and dipped her roller into the paint in the pan, then went for the attack on the giraffes. Each stroke was both somber and exhilarating. She felt wistful as the remnants of his childhood were erased under the brilliant white paint. But she also felt the anger of unfairness radiating through her and powering the movements of the roller. Soon she was slapping the paint on the walls, breathing heavy with each roll. She moved quickly, the green disappearing as the white enveloped the room. The giraffes were obliterated. Soon, there was nothing to see but white walls between the ceiling and the plush tan carpet.

"Wow, you've been busy," Michael said from the doorway, catching her off guard. She turned with a start, paint roller in hand, her breath coming out in short pants as if she'd been running a marathon. "Are you sure you should be working that hard, with your arm the way it is?" he asked.

Jill looked down at her cast. White paint was splattered on the dingy white of her cast and on her light blue sling. She looked back at Michael, feeling her anger evaporating into the naked walls. She gave him a sheepish grin.

"I may have overextended myself a little today," she admitted. She could feel her arm throbbing, her pain pill still lying in the container on the kitchen counter. By the rumble in her stomach, she realized she'd also forgotten to eat.

"Come on," he laughed, stepping into the room to take the paint roller from her. "You go call for some take-out for dinner, and I'll get this cleaned up."

"But your suit," Jill argued. He looked down at his navy blue jacket and pants.

"Okay, after I change I'll clean this up."

They didn't even bother with plates, eating straight out of the Chinese food containers with chopsticks. Michael passed Jill the sweet and sour pork, and she picked around the pineapple to reach the meat in red sauce. They sat on the floor of the bedroom, now empty of everything that was once in it. It was left a clean slate, ready to become whatever they wanted it to be.

"So, what's your plan for this room?" Michael asked before taking another bite of Chow Mein.

"I'm not sure," Jill said, surveying the space in the room. It seemed so much bigger than before. The backseat of her car now held every item she could bear to give up. She wondered if she was making a mistake, knowing that once it was all gone…it would be *gone*. But each time she felt herself waffling, she pushed it out of her mind, choosing to go through the motions instead of thinking with her heart. To stop the momentum threatened to lead her back to the darkness…back to the couch.

"Well, we could make it a second bedroom for guests," Michael suggested. "Or maybe an office, or an art studio." Jill perked up at the last idea.

"An art studio," she repeated, mulling it over. Before Toby had been born, she had spent many hours each day on different forms of creation—from clay sculptures to paintings, fabric collages to watercolors, glass jewelry to pottery, and everything in between. She'd even garnered the interest of a few boutiques and studios, and managed to make a small amount of money from sales. But with Toby's arrival came a crunch on her creative time and desire. She traded in her art brushes for mommyhood, her time devoted more to raising a baby than being able to be alone with her art. "Possibly. We'll have to take the carpet out first, though."

"It wouldn't be that hard to do," Michael said, surveying the carpet. "We could lay down Pergo in an afternoon, easy." He looked back at her and smiled. "I've got to say, it's strange to see the room so empty."

"Are you mad?" Jill asked. "I should have checked with you, I know. But I just felt like this room was holding me back so much."

"No, it makes sense. With everything still in here, we were only keeping the door closed, anyway. What's your plan for his things?"

"I was going to donate the majority of it," Jill said. "But I don't know if we'll regret it once it's all gone." She studied his expression, searching for any sign of disagreement on his part. She couldn't read him, though. "I did save a small box of items I couldn't bear to give up," she added in. He looked up and smiled with a nod.

"I did, too," he admitted. "The night Toby died, I pulled a few things out while I was cleaning. They're in a box in the attic. The rest of his things, however, I couldn't bring myself to do anything with. I knew we'd never use any of it, even if we decide to have another child."

"Do you think we will?" she asked. "I mean, have another baby?"

"I don't know," Michael said. "I mean, I hope we do."

"Me too," Jill said. They both left the conversation at that, eating for a few minutes in silence to avoid a topic neither of them was ready to broach.

"So, did you have a chance to look for a job today?" Michael asked. Jill shook her head.

"No, this kind of took up all my time. Sorry," she said.

"You don't need to apologize, Jill. Remember, you're not doing this because you have to work. You're doing this because you want to."

"I know. It's just that….well, it's scary. And…"

"And what?" he asked.

Jill could feel her eyes well up with tears, and she did her best to fight them. But it was no use. Her face crumpled as the gravity of the day, the week, the past three months weighed upon her. She looked around the room. "I think I made a mistake. The room, it's too empty. We can't have another child. I can't go back to work. It's all happening too fast. It's like we're pretending he never existed. How can I just go on living when he doesn't get to?"

"Hey! It's all going to be okay!" Michael insisted. He set his food container down and crawled over to her, pulling her close. "You're not a bad mother."

"I'm not even a mother anymore," she cried.

"Yes, you are," he corrected her. "Losing Toby doesn't take that away from either of us. We are still his parents, and we always will be."

"But his room…"

"Please, Jill, don't go back there."

Jill jerked her head up and searched his face, her heart plummeting when she saw the graveness in his expression.

"Back where?" she sniffled.

"Back to the place where you couldn't leave the couch, carry on a conversation, or even eat a decent meal. I need my wife back." He said it with such conviction, his own eyes filling with tears. The meaning behind his words hit her like a ton of bricks.

"Oh my God," she whispered. "You were going to leave me."

"No!" he told her, taking her face in his hands. "I wasn't going to leave. But I did wonder how our marriage was going to last. We weren't talking. We were barely even looking at each other. I didn't know how to help you, let alone how to deal with my own grief over this. We were drifting apart, and it scared me to death."

"I don't know what to do, Michael," Jill said through her tears. "I'm not even sure where I am or how I'm supposed to be. I know I didn't belong on the couch, unable to do anything but lay there. But I keep going back and forth over whether I'm a horrible person for wanting to move on. Sometimes I think it would even be easier if I just forgot Toby altogether. But I can't, and I never would. But where's the in-between in all of this? What does it even look like?"

"I don't know," Michael admitted. "I've been in a fog the past several months. Sometimes I feel like I'm just sleepwalking through the day just to survive. But I have to go to work. I have to hold it all together and not just give up, because we have to have an income and a roof over our heads. But there have been several times when I just wanted to walk out of that office, unable to cope with people's petty problems. How could anyone complain to me when their worlds were still intact? I mean, for chrissake, our child had died and they wanted to know why their ad wasn't bringing in more business? It took all I had not to slam the phone down at some of the ridiculousness of their demands. I almost had to pretend our son hadn't died just to get through the day." He wiped his eyes. His face appeared to have taken on a decade of years, and he looked down at Jill with such sadness, her heart broke all over again. "I don't know what the in-between looks like. But I do know I want to find out with you, not without you."

Jill buried her face into his chest, pulling him closer to her so that she could feel his heart beating against her cheek. They stayed silent for a moment, resting against each other as the words lingered in the stark room. It was Jill who finally broke the silence.

"Maybe it's just a matter of admitting that we're sad," she said. "Maybe it's just remembering the beautiful child Toby was, and honoring him by living."

She knew it wasn't going to be that simple, but she felt like maybe, with time, it could be. She also knew how much closer she felt to Michael upon discovering that he was struggling, too. All this time she had felt like he was so strong in being able to continue living instead of dying alongside their son—like she had every day since. Thinking he could cope while she couldn't had made him feel worlds away to her, like he had left her behind in her personal world of darkness. To discover that he had been battling his own grief was eye opening. It gave him a new persona of strength. They could get through this together. She wasn't alone, and neither was he.

She looked up at him, and he pulled away so that he could see her face. Slowly, he leaned down and touched his lips to hers, offering her the lightest of touches that sent a warm jolt of electricity through her veins. The containers of Chinese food were forgotten on the carpet as he pulled them both to a standing position, holding her close as their kiss deepened. This time, neither one of them wavered from their desire. Michael broke from her, taking Jill's hand and leading her to the bedroom. She stood still as he took one piece of clothing off of her at a time, then kept eye contact with her as he undressed himself. Then he made slow and careful love to her as if they were seeing each other for the very first time.

And in a way, they were.

Jill

~ Fourteen ~
Green and Purple Squares

Michael kissed Jill goodbye as she sat at the kitchen table, giving her a quick wink as he grabbed his coffee cup and headed out the door.

"Have a good day, sweetheart," she said before he closed it, smiling at the bounce in his step before she went back to the newspaper in front of her. The classified ads lay in neat black and white rows across the page, with job opportunities boasting of competitive salaries and friendly work environments. But none of them seemed to suit her. She searched for a job that would appeal to her artistic side, but found nothing. She circled a nanny position until she realized it required fluency in German, Spanish, and French on top of English, a Bachelors in child psychology, and was only offering minimum wage. She quickly crossed it out. Beyond not being qualified for the low paying job, she wasn't sure she really wanted to watch someone else's kid. A position for a clothing store manager popped out at her. But as she circled it, she had a brief flashback to her teenage years of working at The Gap, snooty customers and hours of folding denim haunting her until she scribbled that one out, too.

Jill put the pen down and sighed, deciding that sitting with the want ads wasn't going to get her a job. She glanced at the clock, figuring the donation site was probably open by now. Perhaps getting out of the house might inspire some ideas on what she could do for work. She grabbed her keys and locked the door behind her.

The man at the donation site seemed more than a little irritated to have to leave his stool inside the truck to help empty out her car, even as Jill explained she couldn't lift anything with just one arm. He carried each item out of the car, lifting bag by bag from the back seat and dropping them on the ground near the back of the truck. A blanket peeked out of one of the bags, the green and purple squares offering a hint to the rest of the blanket. Jill leapt forward and pulled at it until it came free.

"Sorry," she said to the man. "This one must have gotten in there by mistake." It was the blanket her grandmother had made for Toby a few months before she passed away. It was one that covered both her and her wriggly newborn as she had nursed him in the rocking chair in the corner of his room. Back then, it offered them both warmth and comfort. Now it offered her memories of two dear angels she hoped to see again. She hugged the blanket to her chest, inhaling the soft sweet scent of fabric softener and baby hair.

"Do you need a receipt?" the man asked, every bit of his posture suggesting that she didn't.

"No, it's okay," she told him. She looked at the bags on the ground as he walked back at the truck. Her heart leapt into her throat as he grabbed each one and threw it into the back with the other bags of donations. This was her last chance to change her mind. All she had to do was speak up, tell him she'd made a mistake, grab the bags back and keep the material remnants of her baby boy safe with her forever. Instead, she turned around and got back into her car, turning the key in the ignition and letting out the breath she'd been holding. *He doesn't exist in those boxes,* she thought to herself. *They are all just things. Keeping them would only stop me from moving forward.* The overwhelming nostalgia that had gripped her was now dissipating. She put the car in drive and pushed her foot on the pedal. She almost didn't see the girl in front of her, her eyes filled with fear. Jill slammed on the brakes, but not before her front bumper kissed the girl's thigh, causing her to lurch to the side, but catching herself just before she fell. Jill threw the car in park and jumped out of the driver's seat.

"Are you okay?" she exclaimed. "I'm so sorry! I didn't see you!" Jill winced when she noticed the girl's pregnant belly. "Oh God, you're pregnant. I am so sorry. Did I hurt you? Can I take you the hospital?"

"I'm fine," the girl muttered. She looked up, and Jill's eyes widened. It was her, the girl from the store. Maddie. But this time she looked different. It had only been a few days, yet her face appeared thinner, her brown eyes dull. It didn't look like she'd changed clothes since the last time Jill had seen her, three days earlier when she was being led away by the police. Her hair hadn't been washed either, and it hung around her face in oily strands.

If Maddie recognized her, she made no signs of it. She turned from Jill as if she didn't even exist, continuing toward the donation truck Jill had just come from.

"Sir, do you have any blankets in there?" she asked the man on the stool. He looked up at the girl, appearing to mull over whether to be generous or not. In the end, he chose the latter.

"We don't give things away, Miss. I'm not really supposed to sell anything here, either. Our store is located a few miles down the road."

"That's too far away," Maddie mumbled. The man sighed and got off his stool. He peered over his shoulder at the bags behind him.

"Tell you what, you give me five dollars, and I'll let you choose something," he said. Her face fell.

"Never mind," she said, and she turned to walk away.

"Wait," Jill said. She reached into her car and pulled out the patchwork quilt. She didn't even think twice before holding it out to the girl. "You can have this."

Maddie looked up, a look of gratefulness washing over her face.

"Thank you," she said, offering Jill a smile. Through the dirt streaks on her face, Jill saw someone's daughter, a girl who was handed a rough lot in life, a child who was forced to grow up too fast. Maddie began to walk away.

"Hold on," Jill said. "Let me give you a little money, too." The girl didn't argue as Jill reached into her purse and pulled out a twenty. She handed it to Maddie, who took it with a dirty hand. Jill couldn't help but notice the light that flashed in the girl's eyes.

"Thank you ma'am," she said, clasping the money and the blanket to her chest. She started to walk away again, but Jill reached out and took her arm. "Ma'am?" Maddie asked, a confused smile on her face.

"Do you remember me?" Jill asked her. Maddie's smile faded, an inquisitive look taking over her expression. She glanced down at Jill's casted arm. Then her eyes widened in recognition. She turned to run, but Jill kept her hold firm on the girl's arm.

"Let me go!" Maddie cried. She pulled at her arm, but Jill held on tight. She finally stopped struggling, but the look of fear remained on her face. Jill loosened her grip, slipping her hand down to the girl's thin wrist.

"Maddie, right?" Jill said. Maddie looked up in surprise at the sound of her name. She took a deep breath in, and then nodded. Then she looked at the money and blanket she was still holding.

"Here," she said, handing them back to Jill.

"No, they're yours," Jill said, letting go of Maddie's wrist and pushing them back toward her. Maddie's forehead crinkled as she regarded Jill.

"Why are you doing this?" she asked. "I tried to take your wallet. I broke your arm. You should be angry with me."

Jill looked at the girl before her. She was right. She should be angry with her. But she wasn't. If anything, this girl had managed to knock loose the walls of pain Jill had surrounded herself with, giving her a desire to seek out her own purpose rather than live in misery.

"Honey, whatever feelings I could have over you stealing from me, or even over this broken arm, are nothing compared to what you've apparently been through," Jill told the girl. She looked at the cash in Maddie's hand, and realized that twenty dollars wasn't nearly enough. "Can I do something for you? Anything? I can take you wherever you need to go. Maybe someone's house? You can't stay out here like this."

"Like what? You mean pregnant?" Maddie laughed at this. "No disrespect, ma'am, but even my own parents don't care that I'm out here. Besides, I'm doing fine. I just earned twenty dollars." She turned to walk away. This time Jill didn't try to stop her. "Thank you for the money," she called back to Jill without turning around. Toby's blanket lay over her shoulders, and Jill watched the green and purple squares disappear with her as she rounded the corner.

Maddie

- Fifteen -
The Turning Point

Maddie huddled just around the corner of a store building and sunk down against the brick wall. Her muscles were fraught with nerves from coming face-to-face with the woman she wanted to forget. The moment had her mentally reliving their first encounter over and over. To Maddie, this woman represented the point where everything went wrong. When she had reached into the woman's purse to grab her wallet, Maddie lost her boyfriend, her security, her parents, and everything that allowed her to survive comfortably. Now she was living on the street, begging for luxuries like unspoiled food and blankets to keep warm—luxuries she had taken for granted only a week ago.

Relaxing her body, she unfurled the blanket from her shoulders and placed it on the ground next to her. She took a deep breath in, then let it out slow. She felt sick with guilt, especially with the woman's money clenched in her hand. Her face now haunted her. Of course, it wasn't like she hadn't thought of the woman before. Being alone the past few days gave her lots of time to go over every single detail of that moment. Worse, she'd had time to think about every instance that had shaped the direction of her life. She thought of the mistake she'd made in even talking about money with Jordan, accelerating the moment when he'd steal from Ben and Julie, forcing them to leave. She thought of how Jordan had abandoned her, leaving her to not only shoulder the blame for their mutual plan, but to also be faced with raising their baby on her own. She was furious with how much she had trusted him. He had manipulated her from the very beginning, taking her innocence and having her believe everything would be okay. He had told her he'd take care of her until the end. Instead, he took off just when things started to go downhill.

But her anger at Jordan was nothing compared to what she felt toward her parents. She could easily dismiss Jordan as a loser. She could tell herself she was better off without him. But her parents? The intensity of her anger made it harder to sleep than the cold concrete that was now her bed. Did she deserve to get kicked out? Maybe. Being alone in her thoughts had given her enough time to look at the situation from all angles. Weeks ago, she'd had the naïve notion that her parents would just support her and the baby, just because she was their daughter. She knew better now. It wasn't their place. She'd made an adult decision, and needed to stand behind it. Getting kicked out of their house still stung, but she forgave them for that. However, this time was different. Here she was, a stranger in a strange town, with no money or place to live. Unlike in Gallup, where friends and a few family members still lived, here she had no one. For her parents to abandon her a second time, leaving her with no protection…it was incomprehensible. They had to have known that Jordan was gone and was never coming back. They had to have known that her options in this town were far more limited than if she'd just stayed in Gallup. Yet, they still left her. Her father's reaction didn't surprise her at all. And while her hatred for him was strong, she hated her mother more. Even if her mother had argued against Maddie being left behind, she never stopped it from happening. She got in the car. She left with her father. For that, Maddie would never forgive her.

Maddie got up from her hiding place and migrated toward the dumpsters in the back of the grocery store. Ironically, it was the same store where Jordan had left her, the one where everything changed. But she didn't know her way around this town, and she still felt too timid to venture further than the parking lot. Plus, in a way, she wanted to be around in case Jordan or her parents had a change of heart. This would be the only place they could find her.

Behind the store was a collection of discarded clothing she'd managed to snag from the donation truck when the collection guy wasn't looking. She didn't want to make stealing a habit, but morals appeared out of place when survival was required. Plus, the clothing made the concrete a bit more bearable at night. She added the blanket to the pile, but then looked around. A few other transients made the parking lot their home. If she left anything worth taking out in the open, it would surely be gone by that evening.

She peered into the dumpster, moving aside some rotting vegetables and a few old magazines until she found a near empty garbage bag. Relieved to find only paper inside, she emptied it and then stuffed the blanket and clothes inside. Then she crossed the lot to an area thick with trees. Looking around again to see if she was being watched, she tossed the bag up on a branch that was reachable from the ground, but still hidden from the public eye.

That's when she saw the old man.

Or rather, she smelled him first. The odor lay somewhere between urine and old beer. She looked to see where it was coming from, and spotted him hiding in the shadows, a bagged bottle in his hand. He was watching her every move. In the three days she'd been there, she wondered how long he had been watching her. Fear gripped her for a moment, wondering if he'd try anything should he have a chance. But a second glance in his direction, and she knew there was nothing to worry about.

He was small in stature, as evidenced by the way he sat huddled against a chain link fence with his knees drawn up to his chest. The hair on his unshaven face lay in white patches over the maze of age lines. A hat was on his head, wisps of thin hair escaping in matted disarray. Despite the summer heat, he wore layers of clothes, as if it were easier just to have them on than to carry them.

"Hello," Maddie said. He shrank back at the sound of her voice, scooting further into the shadows as if it would make him invisible. "I don't want to bother you," Maddie said. "My name is Maddie. What's yours?" He didn't speak to her; he just looked away, appearing to hope she'd leave.

Maddie took the hint. "Okay, sir. I'll go now. But I'm hiding my stuff here. You're welcome to a few of the clothes, if you want. But please leave the blanket for me." He continued to look away. But Maddie swore she could see the expression on his face soften.

With her twenty dollars in hand, Maddie got up and walked toward the supermarket. She hadn't been in there since the incident, choosing instead to chance the leftover food thrown away each night behind the Mexican restaurant. She wondered if anyone inside would notice her. With her heart pounding, she slipped through the sliding doors, peering toward the register to see if the cashiers were watching her. They all were, to her dismay— at least out of the corner of their eyes. She realized they were looking at her as if she were just one of the random homeless people outside, and not the thief she had been. Maddie relaxed, refusing to be bothered by their discrete stares. She wandered the aisles, searching for something worth buying as her stomach complained. With one hand on her belly, she reached forward to grab a granola bar off the shelf. But when she saw how dirty her hands were, she thought better of it, especially when she noticed the grimace on a woman's face as she shopped a few feet away. *You touch it, you buy it,* Maddie thought, hiding her hands in her pockets.

She found a pre-made sandwich in the deli area, and a large bottle of water in the refrigerated section. She grabbed a box of crackers and then took her finds to the cash register to pay. After collecting her change, she returned to the back of the building and sat under the tree.

She wouldn't look at the man directly, but Maddie could see that he was still there in the shadows. She tore her sandwich in half and placed it on a napkin close to where she sat, then pulled it so that it was closer to him. Holding her breath, she waited to see if he'd take the bait. But only the breeze touched it, ruffling the napkin it sat on.

Maddie bit into her own half of the sandwich, her eyes closed as the flavor of ham between bread found its way into the emptiness of her stomach. Never had anything tasted so good. She concentrated on taking small bites, now regretting her small offering to the man that remained where she placed it, untouched. But to take it back now would be wrong; certainly he knew it was for him.

Her sandwich was gone too soon, and she compensated by drinking a huge gulp of water before starting in on the crackers. Once the salty crispness hit her tongue, she knew she could eat the whole box in one sitting. But she restrained herself to finishing off just one of the four wrapped sleeves in the box. She downed another swig of water, then capped it to save for later. Then she gathered her food and placed it in the tree next to her bag. Eyeing the lonely sandwich, she walked away from the tree and counted to sixty. One one thousand. Two one thousand. Three one thousand... Sixty one thousand. She turned around and crept back toward the tree. The napkin the sandwich had been on fluttered upwards in a gust of wind, dancing upon the breeze as it was carried higher and higher into the sky. Peeking down, she could only see the tips of the man's feet underneath the tree. But he moved them back and forth as if enjoying something really good.

Jill

~ Sixteen ~
Saving the Girl

"I saw her today," Jill mumbled into her tea. Michael settled down on the couch next to her, moving carefully so that the hot liquid didn't jump from her cup.

"Saw who?" he asked. He had the remote in his hand, poised to turn on the TV. But he must have noticed her troubled expression because he set the remote down and gave her his full attention. "What's up, babe? Want to talk about it?"

"I saw that girl. Maddie. The one who tried to steal my wallet." She kept her cup of tea close to her lips, but only inhaled the steam, waiting until it was cool enough to drink.

"So what was her deal?" he asked. "Did she pull anything funny?" He paused and shook his head. "I'm surprised she's even out and about. You'd think her parents would have her under lock and key after that stunt she pulled. At the very least, they owe us a phone call or something." He eyed her casted arm with meaning, then looked back at her with raised eyebrows.

"Thing is, I don't think she has any parents," Jill said. "In fact, I don't think she has a home. When I saw her today, she was asking the guy at the donation truck for a blanket to keep warm. Michael, she looked so thin, I could barely tell she was pregnant. And it's only been a few days! She was dirty, and I swear she was wearing the same clothes I saw her in three days ago." Jill winced, remembering the fight the girl possessed when the officers were arresting her. But this afternoon, all that fight was gone. It was like her spirit had left her, like she'd given up all hope.

"So what are you thinking?" Michael asked. Her eyes shot open and she peered at her husband's face. He sighed, his eyebrows raised. "Come on, Jill. I can see the wheels turning in your head. Out with it."

"I'm afraid to say. It's stupid." She blew on her tea some more, trying to avoid answering him.

"You don't want to bring her here, do you?" he asked. Jill kept her eyes trained on her tea as she nodded yes. Michael sighed again, shaking his head. "Oh sweetheart," he said. "Your heart is just too kind." Jill looked up at him, wondering if it as a compliment or not. He held a troubled look in his eyes. "Okay, let's say she moves in here," he said. "I supposed she would take the guest room, right?"

"That's what I was thinking," Jill said. She put the tea down on the table, the weight lifting off her shoulders as Michael plotted out the scenario.

"That means we'll have to get her a new bed, and likely some new clothes. Probably a crib for the coming baby too, right?" Jill nodded, but felt her shoulders sag as she saw where he was going with this. "Then we'll have to enroll her in school around here and sign her up for medical insurance. Do you think we can even do that, being that she's likely a runaway who probably already has legal guardians?" Jill shrugged, looking down at her lap. "Let's say we work all that out, and now she's living with us. What if she messes up, like gets into trouble or does drugs? What if she steals again? What if she steals from us? How will we handle that? What if it gets so bad that you want her gone? Will you kick her out?"

Jill blinked rapidly to keep the tears at bay as Michael gave her a heavy dose of reality. She knew it was all stuff she had to think about. But that didn't mean she *wanted* to think about it.

"I don't know, Michael. I just can't see how I can come across her like that and just walk away without doing anything. I mean, she's pregnant! This can't be good for her or the baby. She's just so young. It seems horrible that her parents would turn their backs on her like this.

"But that's the thing, Jill. We don't even know why her parents won't take care of her. What if she's done something awful? What if there's some serious reasons why she's on the streets?"

"I just...." Jill started, trying to find the words that could prove her point. They weren't there. "I just don't see it," she finished.

"But you don't–" he started, but she cut him off.

"What, know her?" she asked. She sat up and turned so she could look him square in the face. "I know I don't know her! But there's something about her I do see. Three days ago, when she was being led away by the cops, our eyes met. There's an innocence inside of her, and it's still there. If she were some hardened criminal, she would have found a way off the streets by now. Instead, she's barely eating, she's sleeping in the elements, and she's going to die if we don't do anything." By this time, her conviction was set. To her, the decision was already made. She didn't know how any of the things Michael mentioned would work out. She wasn't sure if she even knew how to raise a teenager, let alone a teenager who would be having a child in a few months. She didn't know what she'd do if this girl were using drugs, if she became violent, or if she stole all their belongings and took off. She didn't even want to think about it. But she felt like she didn't have to. If she brought this girl home, she'd be safe from the streets and heal from whatever travesties life had thrown at her. The rest of the stuff could be dealt with one at a time, as necessary.

"Jill, I know you're determined," Michael said gently, taking her hands in his. "And I know you don't want to hear it. But there's more we need to think about. We have no idea how long this girl has been living on the streets. She most likely hasn't been getting proper medical care, or even eating well for months. There's a possibility this has affected her child. If her child lives, it could have severe problems. And if she's under our care and the baby dies, it might feel like losing Toby all over again."

"I know," she admitted, looking at their hands intertwined in her lap. "I've kind of thought of that already. But if I do nothing, I'll feel like anything bad that happens to her from here on out will be all my fault."

Michael looked away, staring at some invisible spot on the wall behind Jill. He blinked hard, his mouth working into a set line as if he were trying to find the right words. Finally, he looked at her. Jill was surprised to see the tears in his eyes.

"Please don't do this," he said, his voice trembled slightly, but he remained composed.

"Do what?"

"This, Jill. I mean, I get it. You feel bad for her. But I just got you back. I'm scared that you're going to get your heart set on going above and beyond to help this girl, and then get your heart trampled in the process. I'm afraid you'll lose yourself again. And if you lose yourself, I'm afraid I'll never find you again."

He managed to keep the tears at bay, but just the presence of them was enough to shake Jill up. They brought her back to understanding she wasn't the only one involved in this decision. But they also stood in the way of her getting what she wanted. She was caught somewhere in the middle of sympathy and frustration, and wasn't sure which emotion was stronger.

"Honey, it's fine," she said, taking his hand. "There's no decision that needs to be made right now. We're just talking. Let's sleep on it tonight, and perhaps there will be a solution in the morning."

Michael sighed. He looked at Jill, and she knew he wanted to argue with her persistence to not put this whole idea to bed. But he only shook his head and gave her a tired smile. Jill smiled back, but she could feel her frustration winning out. She lingered in the living room as Michael got up to go to bed, resolving to compose herself before following him to their room. But once he left, her frustration turned to anger. *What was he thinking?* She had already known that he wasn't going to agree wholeheartedly to her idea. And it wasn't like she was going to go out that night, find Maddie, and bring her home. But his resistance still felt like an unnecessary roadblock.

And then there were the tears.

She knew it was hypocritical to even let them get to her. Up until recently, she had been the crier and he had been the strong one. But she felt like, this time, he only cried to get her to stop talking about it. And it had worked. Once his emotions got between them, the conversation had come to a halt. Jill felt like a horrible person to be so callous to his feelings. She knew the dangers of losing herself in trying to save Maddie, just like she had lost herself over Toby's death. Michael's fears were valid and true.

But overwhelming all of this was her worry over Maddie and the situation this young girl was in. The longer she did nothing, the longer Maddie remained vulnerable to the dangers of the world. Each passing moment made Jill feel that much more responsible for the girl, and Michael's resistance seemed like a betrayal.

Jill went to bed that night still angry. Michael was already asleep when she crept into the room, his back facing her side of the bed. She shed her clothes and slipped in between the covers, moving so that she didn't disturb him while he slept. As she listened to him breathe, she could feel her anger dissolving. The man she married had a good heart, but he also had a good head on his shoulders. To him, family always came first. Jill sighed, coming to the realization that Michael wasn't being callous to Maddie's predicament; he was being protective over *her*—his wife. She rolled over and faced his back, watching his shape rise and fall in the moonlight that streamed in from the window. Maneuvering her good hand out from underneath her, she reached over and touched him. He breathed in sharp, then let it out, still asleep. Jill moved closer and curled into him, her casted arm resting against the top of her body while her other remained on his back. She felt him shift against her, molding himself to her shape.

"I love you, honey," he murmured.

"I love you, too," she whispered.

That night, Jill's dreams were filled with visions of Maddie. Every time she drifted off, Maddie would stand before her. Her face was stained with tears and dirt, her eyes large above her gaunt cheekbones, her hands embracing her stomach. Her face was contorted with anguish, wordlessly begging Jill to help her with the panic in her eyes. Jill tried to reach out to her, but she couldn't seem to get close enough to touch her. *Help me,* the girl mouthed, her face twisting into a silent scream. Jill ran forward, putting her arms out to try and reach her. Finally she got hold of Maddie's pink sweatshirt. But when she pulled, Maddie and the sweatshirt both vanished into thin air. Everything around Jill evaporated, and she pitched forward into darkness.

Jill lurched forward, waking in her bed.

"Ow!" Michael yelped as her cast hit him in the arm.

"Sorry," she whispered. They rolled away from each other, and she felt him settle back into sleep. She moved so that her casted arm was free from underneath her, the blankets shifting to her waist in the process. Despite it being July, the night air of the house had a slight chill to it. She started to move the blankets back over her, but then paused. Maddie was out there in the cold, Toby's blanket her only protection from the night. Jill pulled the blanket completely off of her, allowing the cool air to engulf her skin. She wanted to feel what Maddie was feeling. But after only five minutes, the chill was too much. She pulled the covers back up to her chin, her resolve to help the pregnant girl stronger than ever. Michael might have balked at her bringing Maddie to their house, but that didn't mean she had to do nothing for the girl.

Sleep eluded Jill as plans spun through her head, swirling around her with no beginning or end. It took almost an hour for her mind to quiet, but when it did, she fell into a dreamless sleep until morning.

Jill

- Seventeen -
The Truth About Bums

Jill rummaged through some boxes stacked along the walls of the garage, searching for unused items she hadn't gotten around to giving away yet. She nabbed a down blanket, one of her old jackets, and a few maternity clothes she had been saving for any future pregnancies. She then went back in the house and made several peanut butter and jelly sandwiches, laying the ingredients on thick between the pieces of bread. She placed these in a paper bag, adding a few bottled waters and a bag of cookies she'd baked earlier that morning. With the bag in her passenger seat, Jill then drove back to the place where she had seen Maddie the day before, parking her car between the grocery store and the donation truck.

The coolness of the night before had disappeared completely, a hot July breeze pushing into the car as soon as Jill rolled down her window and looked around the lot. Back-to-school signs hung from the light posts despite there being another month until classes would be in. Jill closed her eyes and breathed in deep, letting it out in a slow, even breath. She would never know what it was like to walk Toby to his first day of school. It was yet another milestone that died with Toby when he was taken from her.

Jill left the air-conditioned coolness of her car to search the parameters of the parking lot. Clutching the paper bag in her good arm, she tried to appear like she was window shopping at the shops that shared the lot with the grocery store. Really, she was searching for any sign that Maddie was there. However, the girl wasn't anywhere out in the open, as Jill soon found out. But judging by a couple of characters begging for change outside storefronts, it appeared that a homeless encampment was nearby.

Seated in a wheelchair outside the pharmacy was an old man wearing a fishing hat, his golden retriever at his feet. The dog wore bunny ears on his head, and the man held a sign that read, "Have a heart for two old dogs." Jill smiled at the man, and almost laughed when the man scowled back. His grumpy face clashed with the silly ears of his dog and the lighthearted sign.

A few stores away was a man wearing ratty clothing with unkempt hair and a scraggly beard, his eyes closed as he strummed the guitar in his lap. His hat lay upside down on the ground, a few dollars scattered inside. While his appearance was gruff, his voice was anything but. Jill paused near a post, halfway hiding behind it as she listened to the gentle way he sang over his melodic playing. She lost herself in the song, forgetting in the moment that a homeless man was the one singing. But as she felt the song coming to a close, she moved to scoot past him, afraid he'd reach his hand out for money in exchange for the show. She was mortified when he opened his eyes just long enough to give her a wink, laughing within the melody as she rushed by.

Jill gave up looking around the storefronts and moved toward the back. There she found an old man sleeping on a pile of clothing underneath a few trees. But there seemed no sign of Maddie. So she moved on toward the donation truck. No one was there, not even the attendant who had been there the day before.

She continued on by the taco truck, avoiding eye contact with the small group of men nearby, waiting for someone to pick them up for a day job. She passed by the mothers with their train of children, pushing their shopping carts into the grocery store. She stopped in the middle of the lot and took one last roundabout look, hoping she might get a glimpse of the girl. But she was nowhere.

Perhaps Michael was right. Perhaps she just went home.

Jill walked back to her car with the bag of food still in her hand. She placed the food on the hood of her car, trading it for the bag of clothing on her backseat. This she left at the donation truck before heading back to her car.

But then there was the food.

She had meant it all to be for Maddie. The food was now just going to go to waste. Jill looked around, peering at the few homeless men around the lot. She took a deep breath and walked back toward the stores. The man in the wheelchair was still there in front of the pharmacy. He scowled as she came closer, but the dog made up for it with a drooling grin.

"Here you go, sir," she said with a smile, feeling timid as she held one of the sandwiches toward him. He glanced at the sandwich, then grunted, looking away. Jill stood there, stunned. She was sure he'd be appreciative of the sandwich, as meager as it was. And yet, he acted as if he was above the simple sandwich. "Aren't you hungry?" she asked him, her smile fading from her face. He kept looking past her, pretending she wasn't even there. But when it became apparent that she wasn't going to leave, he snorted through his nose and turned to glare at her.

"Money," he blurted out in a thick voice.

"Excuse me?" Jill stammered. He leaned forward, causing Jill to take a step back.

"Do. You. Have. Any. Money." He pronounced each word slow, as if Jill lacked the intelligence to understand him. She placed her casted arm on the purse slung over her shoulder and shook her head no, hoping it wasn't obvious that she did have a few dollars—just not for him. She was still holding the sandwich in her hand, the weight of it beginning to feel like lead. Once again, she held it out to him, though all she really wanted to do was walk back to her car and drive away, forgetting about her whole stupid idea of helping anyone.

"Sir, would you please take the sandwich," she said, her voice wavering as she waited for him to reach for it. "I just made it this morning." The man stared at her for a moment, then let out a sigh as if he were about to do her a huge favor. He held out a dirty hand, and Jill placed the sandwich in it, eyeing his black fingernails and oily skin. He took the sandwich out of the plastic bag, which he handed back to her. Then he tossed the sandwich into the dog bowl near his golden retriever. The dog sprang to life, his bunny ears bobbing up and down as he wolfed down the sandwich.

Burning with hurt and anger, Jill spun around and stalked back to her car. She tossed the bag of food in the seat next to her, hearing the satisfying crash as it hit the passenger side door. Just as she was about to get in, she noticed the man with the guitar watching her. He smiled and waved, but she averted her gaze. When she glanced up again, he was still watching her with a wide smile. Then he pointed at her. Jill looked behind her, then back at the man. His grin widened. He then moved his hands to his mouth, pantomiming an eating motion. He wanted food.

Jill sighed. It was the last thing she wanted to do. But she still reached into her car and grabbed the bag off the floorboards where it had fallen, and then brought it over to him.

"Well, what have you got there?" the man asked, his eyes twinkling. Jill felt her face redden as she reached into the bag and pulled out a squished sandwich, handing it to the man.

"Sorry, it was in better condition a few moments ago," she said. He laughed, his voice ringing through her embarrassment and pulling a smile from her. But she had to look away when he slid the sandwich out of the bag and took a generous bite. Her mission had felt so noble that morning. Now she just felt ridiculous.

"This has got to be the best food I've had all week," the man said, his mouth still full from food. He took a swig of water from the bottle she offered, and then motioned to look further in the bag. She handed it to him and let him rifle through it, not even caring about the condition of his dirty hands. She sat down on the bench a couple feet away and leaned back so she could stare up at the blue sky. She was determined to just count the clouds until she was finally free to leave.

"Hey," the man said, peering into Jill's face. "You okay there?" Jill jerked her gaze from the clouds and looked at him, giving him a quick smile.

"I'm fine," she said, but the waver in her voice gave her away. She looked back at the parking lot, biting the inside of her cheek to keep the tears from following, and frustrated when they came anyway. "I'm sorry. This is so stupid," she said.

"What's stupid?" the man asked. He bit into one of the cookies she had, waiting for her to talk.

"This," Jill said. "Me. My stupid plan to save some girl without a home, and that giving someone food could actually be easy."

"Hey, *I* like your food," the man protested. Jill smiled in spite of herself. "Don't let that old codger get you down," he said, nodding his head toward the man in the wheelchair. It seemed he had seen the whole thing. "I'm Oliver Stamps, by the way." He didn't offer his hand in greeting, seeming to understand the unspoken barrier between those with a home, and those without.

"I'm Jill," she said. "You play beautifully," she added in, suddenly feeling shy. She wanted to say more than that, how the sound of his voice was meant for a concert hall, not the streets of Petaluma. But everything she rehearsed in her head felt forced. So she left it at that, smiling down into her lap.

"Thanks," he replied. "And you make a damn good sandwich. Too bad Albert over there wasted it on the dog. His loss." He finished the last bite, sitting back with a satisfied sigh with his hand on his belly.

"I don't get it, Oliver. Why wouldn't he want food? Has he eaten already or something?"

"Nah, not likely," Oliver said, peering up the sidewalk to where Albert was sitting. "It's possible, I guess. I haven't been watching him or anything. But it's a safe bet that man hasn't put anything solid in his stomach all day. Now liquid? That's another story. He's probably out of booze and just needs some poor sap like you, no offense, to give him the means to get it." The guitar was back in Oliver's lap, and he strummed it as he spoke, picking at the strings without putting much thought into it.

"See, this is why I don't give bums money," she said. Then she wanted to crawl into the earth. She looked at Oliver, wondering if he noticed. If he was offended, he didn't show it. Instead, his face held an amused look on it. "Ugh, I'm sorry. I didn't mean the way that sounded," Jill said, her cheeks burning under his gaze.

"No worries," Oliver said, going back to strumming his guitar. "But I feel it my civic duty to clear up some misconceptions for you regarding money and us bums." There was no sign of contempt in his voice as he said it, though, in her shame, Jill knew he was about to give her an education. "First of all, people who give their money to those of us on the streets seem to have delusions that they can tell us how to spend it. But I never told them to give me that money. I may have sought after it by keeping my hat on the ground, or sometimes even outright asking. But I never made them put that money in my hand. That was their choice. Once they parted with that money, their control of it ends. And yet, I have had people tell me to use it wisely, to not buy booze with it, or even giving it to me while saying I'm probably just going to use it on alcohol. I may be the one on the streets begging for handouts, but who's the low-life in this situation? The one asking for help? Or the one giving it with conditions, judgment, or both?" His voice rose as he spoke, still maintaining a peaceful quality, but proving how passionate this subject was to him. He took another drink of water and swallowed, replacing the cap before continuing. "The ones that get me are those that say 'Get a job,' as if getting a job were so easy. I look around and see tons of people out of work, complaining about the job market. I read the papers, I know how bad it is for everyone. Tell me, how is someone like me going to walk into an office building and ask for a job? Are they going to accept these clothes I'm wearing as my suit, and the skills I have of holding my hand out as my reference? What about Albert over there? The guy is so loony, he's mistreating his dog's dignity with those damn rabbit ears." A laugh escaped Jill's lips, and Oliver grinned. "And you know what he has to look forward to?" he continued. "Not a goddamn thing. Every day is the same. He has his dog. He has the clothes on his back. He has Lord knows what in those bags he carries around on his wheelchair. But pleasure? You're looking at it. Luxuries? Nothing more than what he's doing right now. For him, booze is the missing ingredient that takes him off that sidewalk and makes things a little more comfortable. It's his perk, much like you probably enjoy treating yourself to common comforts you're accustomed to. His daily dose of alcohol is like your morning cup of coffee. Sometimes it's the only thing worth living for. Plus, a little shot of brandy can warm anyone on the coldest winter day." He paused, seeming to search Jill's face for an argument. She kept silent, not about to give him one. "The dude has nothing to look forward to. Nothing. And he gets judged for having alcohol as his vice? Hell, there are married men out there addicted to porn or cheating on their wives. There are teens stealing from the stores. Women are talking smack about their husbands behind their backs, or spending family money on useless items. And they all have a roof over their head. But Albert? He sleeps in the cold every night. Least he should be allowed is one bad habit, right?"

"I guess it makes sense," Jill said. "Actually, it makes a lot of sense. But I still don't understand why he wouldn't take food from me. I mean, he just gave it to his dog."

"Were you not listening when I mentioned the bunny ears? Dude's crazy!"

Jill doubled over in laughter, then started to gather her things to leave.

"Hold up, girl. I haven't heard your story yet, starting with that broken arm."

"Not much to say," Jill said. She pointed toward Food Mart, just across the parking lot. "I broke it right over there when a young girl tried to take my wallet."

"Oh, you're the one!" Oliver exclaimed. "I saw the whole thing. And now you're back. Are you trying to catch that girl or something?"

"Not exactly. I'm trying to help her."

"That seems odd, seeing that she got the best of you," he said, nodding at Jill's cast.

"I have this feeling she's not a bad person, but that she just got into a bad situation. I think she's in some kind of trouble." She noticed the way he looked at her, as if she'd just stated the obvious. "Not with the cops. As far as I know, everything's been handled. And I didn't press any charges. But I think she's out here alone. When she tried to steal my wallet a few days back, she was with someone. But he took off without her. From what I can tell, she has no one here—no parents or anything."

"She's that pregnant girl, right? The young one?"

"Yes!" Jill exclaimed. "You've seen her? You know where she's at?"

"I've seen her. She's kind of hard to miss, being a girl sleeping out here among all us old farts. I try to mind my own business, but I can't help but be concerned for her as well, what with her being with child." He scanned the lot for a moment, but then turned to Jill and shrugged. "Can't say I've seen her today, though. It's possible she got work or something."

"Work?" Jill couldn't help her surprise. Who would hire a pregnant teen?

"Yeah. In the mornings, a bunch of the Hispanics hang out by the taco truck, waiting for someone who needs a bit of manual labor done. Usually it's just men, but I've seen a few ladies wait there, probably for housework or something. Your mama-to-be may have caught on to the lay of the land and gotten picked up for some work."

"But she's not Hispanic," Jill pointed out.

"You don't have to be Hispanic to be desperate for work," Oliver said. "Or maybe she just found another spot to stay. That's the difference between us old guys and these young kids who find themselves in our shoes. While we like to stay put, they tend to roam free from one place to another. I reckon she's in the next town by now, probably caught a ride near the freeway."

Oliver went back to strumming his guitar, looking down at his fingers while he played. He began humming with the tune, eventually breaking into song as if Jill wasn't sitting there next to him.

She closed her eyes, feeling her heart sinking. Maddie might be gone. It wasn't like losing Toby, but it was a loss nonetheless. She could feel a small crowd forming around them as Oliver played, and she took the moment to slip away. She looked back just before the crowd closed in on him, catching sight of his wink as he bid her goodbye without breaking from song. As she walked away, she was surrounded by the echo of his corridor concert resonating up and down the concrete walkway, all from a man with a weathered appearance and an angelic voice.

Maddie

- Eighteen -
Survival Mode

She'd been rummaging through the donation bags by the truck when she saw the woman roll into the parking lot. Maddie didn't know what it was that fed this woman's persistence. All she knew was that she wished this woman would just stay the hell away. And so Maddie left the Food Mart parking lot, walking a few miles up the road to find someplace where she could grab a bite to eat and rest for a while until the lady gave up and left.

With the few dollars left in her pocket, she bought three burgers at the first fast food joint she came to, eating just one and saving the rest for later. Then she vacated to a nearby park where she watched people walk by, waiting until she thought enough time had passed. It occurred to her that she could go anywhere, and do anything. She wasn't forced to stay in that parking lot forever. But several hours later, she made the trek back to the parking lot, her feet feeling like lead with each step.

The light was just starting to dim once she arrived, the streetlights turning on one by one. Maddie's stomach rumbled as she held on to the two hamburgers and made her way over to the area behind the Mexican restaurant. She knew this was all she was going to eat, unable to bring herself to rifle through the garbage again for food. She missed the taste of just-cooked meals. She couldn't remember the last time she actually sat at a table to eat, and she felt nostalgic over the dinners she and her parents had ceremoniously shared.

Her parents were starting to feel like strangers, her life with them seeming like someone else's. Yet, she couldn't help but wonder if they thought of her, or if they had let the thought of her go as soon as they rounded the corner and drove away. By now they were probably at home, back into their daily routine. Maybe they chose to forget they even had a daughter at all. Had they cleared out her room? Thrown away all her things? Erased the memory of her from the house once and for all? What did they say to anyone who asked them where she was? Did they say anything at all? Did anyone even care enough to ask?

Maddie pulled the garbage bag full of clothes down from the tree, laying out the items on the ground to resemble a cushioned bed. She took the patchwork quilt and laid that over the clothes, pretending she was actually making a real bed and not just a makeshift one out of people's rejected belongings. Then she sat on the bed and pulled both of the hamburgers out. Her stomach rumbled again, and she placed her hand over her rounded belly in an effort to quiet it.

That's when she felt it—a light flutter against the palm of her hand.

"Whoa," Maddie whispered. Her hunger was momentarily forgotten as she stayed as still as possible, waiting for the baby to kick at her hand again. It didn't take long. She realized the rumblings she'd been feeling all day were just her baby's movements. "You're really in there, aren't you," she whispered to her belly. The baby's kicks fluttered as if answering, and Maddie grinned. It made this all the more real, that she was going to be a mom.

Across the way, the old man was rifling through the garbage can, searching for something to eat. Maddie unwrapped her hamburger and watched him, chewing the cold food slowly to make each bite last longer, keeping her free hand resting on her belly. Was that going to be her one day, searching though garbage for her dinner, night after night? She had no money left. Where would her next meal come from? She looked forlornly at the last of her hamburgers. She knew she should save it, but she was too hungry. She looked at the old man, now picking at the food he found among the trash, eating the parts Maddie hoped weren't spoiled. She could give him her last burger. But she didn't want to. This might be the last good food she had to eat. So she turned away from the old man, unwrapping the final burger with a weight of guilt on her shoulders. And she nibbled at it, even though she wanted to inhale the meal. When it was gone, she crumpled up the wrappers and laid them by her bed, then curled up under the blankets. It wasn't yet dark, but she had nothing else to do. It occurred to her that she could sit outside the stores and beg for money. But that thought made her nervous. Any thought of drawing attention to her made her nervous. She didn't want anyone to see her like this—pregnant, dirty, and without pride.

The night got cooler, the winds of Petaluma sweeping through the parking lot and skimming over Maddie where she slept. The blanket that covered her helped to ward off some of the cold. But it wasn't thick enough to keep her warm. What would winter be like? Would she still be out here? Maddie pulled the covers closer, curling her body into a tight ball in efforts to generate some heat. She hid her face under the blanket, breathing through her mouth to try and add warmth to her cocoon. She could hear the rustling of the old man settling in nearby. Though he was small and frail, his mere presence made Maddie feel a little safer. At the very least, she felt less alone. It didn't matter that he wouldn't speak to her, let alone look at her. He was there, experiencing the same discomfort she was. Or maybe he was used to it. Would she ever get used to this?

Finally warm enough, Maddie peeked her face out from the blankets and watched the last bit of light leave the sky. The wind hit her face, and she closed her eyes, feeling it cool against her exposed skin. She could hear the sounds of traffic echoing throughout the town, a symphony of honks and sirens against a backdrop of engines rushing along the highway. She could feel sleep washing over her, its heavy grasp coaxing her out of consciousness and into dreamland. She kept her hand resting on her belly, the baby's movements rolling through her. She smiled, curling even tighter into herself in her happiness. Everyone may have abandoned her. But she wasn't alone. Even if the old man withered away, the baby was with her always. At least there was that.

Maddie woke the next morning with a start. The sun was just cresting between the buildings, its bright light beaming upon her. She sat up, sore from the hard ground. Her stomach ached from hunger. She placed her hand on her belly, but it was still. She knew she needed to eat. But more than that, she knew the baby needed her to eat. Suddenly, survival took on a whole new meeting. It was no longer just her needs she had to worry about.

A glance over her shoulder, and she could see the old man was still asleep. Maddie crept out of her bed and found a space to relieve herself, hoping the man would stay asleep for the few moments of privacy she needed. When she was done, she went back to her bed and rolled everything into the garbage bag, hiding it in the tree. She hoped she wasn't too late.

Maddie emerged from behind the building, smoothing her clothes and hair as if it would help her appearance. A few groups of men stood near the taco truck, chatting with each other as they waited for rides out of the parking lot. Maddie had seen it often enough in New Mexico to know they were probably getting work. At home, it was usually landscaping or construction. She figured it was probably more of the same here, but perhaps more glamorous than working in the desert.

The past few mornings she had eyed them, wondering if she could do the same. On this day, however, they were the ones eyeing her. The conversations stopped as she settled on the concrete wall that lined the parking lot, and she could feel her skin burning under the weight of their stares. But she kept her head held high, staring straight ahead, hoping she wouldn't make a further fool of herself by not getting hired.

A truck pulled up, a few men already in the cab. They snickered when they caught sight of Maddie, but the driver shushed them. It didn't stop a few chuckles from the men around her, however. A few of them were chosen from the lineup, leaving Maddie behind with those rejected. A few more trucks came and went after that. Some barely noticed her. Others gave her the same amused treatment as the first. Not one of them chose Maddie to get in the car.

She was the last one standing when a Cadillac pulled up. An older man was driving, but it was the elderly woman in the passenger seat who leaned forward and called to Maddie through the man's open window.

"Are you looking for a job?" the woman called out, her frail voice ringing through the air. Maddie nodded, the hopefulness inside her bursting at the seams. From her place on the concrete wall, she peered inside the Cadillac to get a better look at who was speaking to her. The woman in the passenger seat appeared delicate, even from within the car. Her hair peeked out from beneath a scarf, her face hidden beneath large sunglasses, and her body was covered in a crocheted shawl. The driver—her husband, Maddie presumed—appeared solid, even at his age. He wore a hat on his head, just like the ones Maddie had seen in the old Fred Astaire movies her father liked to watch. And he had a kind smile on his face. Something in his expression pulled at Maddie, reaching into her and grabbing hold of the part of her that yearned for a father. She brushed it aside immediately, feeling silly over this impulsive emotion regarding a stranger.

"How are you at washing floors?" the lady asked. Maddie nodded again. She stood up from the wall and approached their car.

"I can clean floors," Maddie said. She held her hands on her belly, but then grew self-conscious and removed her hand. If they thought she was too pregnant, they might not hire her.

"And windows?"

Maddie nodded as the woman listed off several more chores, ready to say yes no matter what was asked of her. She may have had only limited experience in cleaning, but she was determined to have this woman believe she was the best housekeeper out there.

The woman looked at the old man in the driver's seat, who only gave her a shrug. Then she turned back to Maddie. "Get on in, honey. I think you'll do just fine." The old man got out of the car and opened the back door, giving Maddie a wink as she slid onto the leather interior and buckled her seatbelt.

They drove through the hills for about twenty minutes, passing vineyards and horse ranches while traveling the windy road. Maddie searched the door for the window lever and pressed it so that the wind would reach her face and hopefully chase away the nausea.

"Slow down, dear, our guest is getting carsick," the woman said. She turned around to look at Maddie. "Do you need us to stop?" she asked. Maddie shook her head, thankful the fresh air was helping. "What's your name, dear?"

"Maddie," she answered, focusing on the road ahead to keep from getting ill.

"I'm Mrs. Winston, and this is my husband, Mr. Winston. It's nice to meet you." She said it as if they were on their way to enjoy a cup of tea instead of a day of cleaning.

They turned into a driveway bordered by vineyards. A fire station stood off to the right, the fire trucks out in front being washed by men in uniform. To their left was a barn, backed by a large pond. The gravel road they were on made the car bump and shake. Maddie's hand flew back to her stomach, and she breathed in and out in slow breaths until they slowed to a stop. She felt her body relax, the sickness washing away from her as she looked out her window to see where they were at.

A two-story home loomed over them. Maddie noted the large number of windows, and wondered if Mrs. Winston expected her to clean all of them. Gardens surrounded the building, and Maddie could smell lavender as soon as she opened the door. Vineyards stretched out around them on all sides. Maddie peered out into the fields, watching a few workers as they shifted from one vine to the next, clipping bunches of grapes with deft movements and placing them in a plastic crate at their feet.

"Harvest has started early this year," Mr. Winston said, noticing where her attention was when he opened her door. "In between whatever my dear wife has planned for you, I'll be requiring some lunches made for the workers. We have about a dozen of them out there today. Mrs. Winston will show you where all the fixings are." Maddie nodded, and followed the old man around the car. He opened the passenger door for his wife, pausing as she found her cane and set it on the road. She took his hand with her other one, and let him help hoist her up.

"Follow Mrs. Winston into the house while I park the car," Mr. Winston said.

The elderly woman crept forward with Maddie in tow. She led Maddie into the foyer, waving one hand around as she showed Maddie the house, her other hand gripping her cane. As the woman barked out instructions on cleaning, Maddie could feel her stomach tied up in knots. Her eyes widened as they passed the laundry room, Mrs. Winston listing off every item that needed to be washed. Maddie had never washed an article of clothing in her life. Even at Julie's house, she had managed to sidestep this particular chore by just washing their clothes in the bathtub when no one was home. The machines just seemed too complicated. She sighed with dread as Mrs. Winston opened the cupboards to show her where the laundry detergent and softener was. But she caught herself before the old woman turned around, nodding with a smile as she kept a mental tally of all her duties. Would there be enough time in the day to get it all done?

"Have you eaten, dear?" the woman asked. Maddie shook her head no. She was led into a giant kitchen filled with bright lights and large windows. In the middle of the kitchen was an island countertop, large copper pans hanging above it. To the side was a large wooden table. Mrs. Winston instructed her to sit there, even though Maddie was the one who was supposed to be working. She began rummaging through the refrigerator. But then, she stopped. She turned and looked at Maddie, all recognition lost from her face.

"I'm sorry, dear. Who are you?" she asked.

It suddenly occurred to Maddie why she was there. She had seen her own grandmother give her these kinds of looks in the months before she lost her memory for good. While Mrs. Winston had led Maddie through the whole house, giving her very detailed instructions on what needed cleaning, she apparently had holes in her memory—the beginnings of dementia.

Maddie sprang to her feet and led Mrs. Winston to the table.

"I'm Maddie, Mrs. Winston. And I was just about to make us both something to eat. Is there anything in particular that you'd like?" She went back to the refrigerator to see what she had to work with. Staring back at her was more food in one place than she had ever seen in her life.

"Oh. Oh dear. I'm sorry, I just forgot. Yes, Maddie, I'd love a sandwich. And after we eat, could you make sandwiches for the workers outside? I think we have two or three of them out there."

Maddie smiled, looking up at the loaves of bread on top of the refrigerator, deciding it wasn't important to correct the woman.

Maddie

- Nineteen -
Not Like Us

Maddie was left alone in the kitchen to clean up after lunch. Her head was already swimming with all that needed to be done. She wished she had taken the time to write it all down, and hoped she would remember it all. She felt an extra burst of energy from the sandwich, and fondly remembered the slices of lettuce she had crunched into with each bite. She had never been a vegetable eater. Now, she craved them. She wasn't sure if it was the baby's doing, or the fact that vegetables weren't readily available to her anymore.

Maddie set to work on the sandwiches for the vineyard workers, using the wide counter space to set out twenty-four slices of bread, and decorating twelve of them with mayonnaise, turkey, and lettuce. She wrapped each one in a napkin, placing them in a basket. She then added twelve apples for good measure. She peered into the refrigerator for something they could drink, but saw nothing. The basket was already heavy enough, as it was. She hoisted it up, feeling the weight of it straining all the way to under her belly. She then lugged it to the sliding glass door that led to the back of the property. There she found herself on a patio. She looked around, seeing green lines of leaves stretching out into the horizon. *Where do I go?* She peered around the enormous landscape of the backyard. When she turned to head back into the house, she caught sight of a worker clipping grapes off one of the nearby vines. Maddie set the basket down, and walked toward him. She felt shy as the man caught sight of her movement and looked up.

"Lunch?" she asked, motioning to the basket she'd left on the patio. He grinned and nodded, then looked back into the fields.

"Hombres! Es hora de almorzar," he called out. Several more men appeared from the vines. She could hear the man's words echoing among the workers throughout the vineyard as they called each other in from the fields. One by one they emerged, grinning with sweaty faces under brimmed hats. Maddie became aware of how meager the sandwich she'd provided them was, embarrassed she hadn't thought to make anything else.

"I'm sorry," she said to the first worker she'd seen. "I hope it's enough."

"Es enough," the man said in broken English, his voice marbling under a thick accent. "Gracias."

"Do you need something to drink?" she asked him. He paused, and she pantomimed bringing a cup to her lips. His face lit up with recognition. He shook his head no, then nodded toward the vineyard. She noticed the large thermos of water that hung from every fifth or sixth line of vines.

The man reached into the basket and pulled out several sandwiches, then passed them out to the workers. Maddie rushed forward to grab the apples, placing them near each worker. They smiled, nodding their silent thanks to her. Unlike the men at the taco stand, they didn't appear to find her presence humorous in the least. They ate in silence, the conversation put on hold as they finished what Maddie had made for them.

She waited until the workers were done and then gathered the garbage from their lunch. The men went back to the vines, and Maddie re-entered the house to get her work done. After cleaning out the basket, she found a pad of paper and made a list of all the things she could remember Mrs. Winston telling her to do.

Sweep and mop floors. Wipe down all surfaces. Scrub the bathrooms. Vacuum the upstairs. Change the sheets on all the beds. Wash, fold, and put away the linens. Cut the vegetables and marinate the meat for that night's dinner. Wash the dishes and put them away.

Maddie rolled up her sleeves and set to work. She found that while she'd never done some of the things on the list, she was still able to find a natural rhythm with the task— except for washing clothes. Once at the washer, Maddie poured in the soap and let the water start the foam in the bubbles. Then she added the linens. But when the bubbles started to emerge from the lid, she knew something was wrong. She picked up the detergent bottle and read the instructions, noting that she'd added five times the recommended amount, possibly more. As the bubbles spilled out of the washer, Maddie grabbed a bucket and prayed Mr. or Mrs. Winston wouldn't walk by and see her mistake. She scooped out the bubbles and poured them into the sink behind her in the washroom. But the bubbles were coming faster than she could contain them. Close to tears, she was getting ready to give up. But then she had another idea. She shut off the washer and pulled out all the soapy material, placing them in a laundry basket. One by one, she rinsed each sheet and blanket in the sink, watching as the bubbles disappeared down the drain. Then she cleaned up what had emerged from the machine. Placing the linens back in the washer, she started over. This time the machine hummed as if in approval.

With limited time, Maddie rushed through prepping dinner, washing the dishes, throwing the linens in the dryer, and mopping the kitchen floor. She ran a vacuum over the carpet upstairs, then folded the dried sheets and blankets before setting them in the linen cabinet. As she put away the clean dishes, Mr. Winston came into the kitchen.

"All done, dear?" he asked. She nodded. He looked around amazed. "Wow, even the windows?" Maddie's face fell. She had forgotten the windows.

"I'm sorry, I forgot," she said. "I can get to them now." Her body ached, but she refrained from wincing as she said it. To her relief, Mr. Winston merely shook his head no.

"It will give you something to do tomorrow," he said with a wink. *Tomorrow.* She was coming back!

She didn't want to leave the bright home or the warmth inside. The thought of returning to her bed of clothing in the parking lot dropped a weight on her shoulders. Still, she followed Mr. Winston out the front door, climbing in the back seat of his car waiting out front. A man she didn't know was sitting in the driver's seat.

"This is Jefferson," Mr. Winston said. "He'll be driving you back home today. You just tell him where you live, and he'll take you there." He handed Maddie some cash, and patted her hand. "You did well," he said. He glanced at her belly, a troubled look crossing his face. But it was gone as soon as it came, replaced with a wide smile.

"Where to?" Jefferson asked, his eyes meeting hers in the rearview mirror.

"The parking lot of Food Mart," Maddie said. He gave her a perplexed look.

"I can take you home, though. It's no trouble.

"I know," Maddie said. "But I promised my mother I'd do a little shopping." His expression wasn't changing, so she added in, "She's picking me up at the store, don't worry."

"All right, miss," he said, though he didn't look convinced.

When they got there, Jefferson pulled the car out front of the supermarket. "Do you want me to wait until your mom gets here?" he asked. Maddie shook her head no.

"I don't know how long I'll be," she said. "It's okay, really. I do this all the time." She flashed him a grin as she opened the door to get out, hoping he'd believe her. "Thank you for the ride." She could feel his eyes watching her as she entered the store, and wondered if he'd remain idle in front the whole time she was shopping. When she was safely out of view, she opened her hand to count the money Mr. Winston had handed her. Thirty dollars. Thirty!

If he kept hiring her, she'd have more than enough money to survive. She might even be able to afford a small place for her and the baby to live.

Maddie went quick through the aisles, her stomach rumbling along with the baby kicking as she found food to eat. She settled on an already roasted chicken, some French bread, and a large salad to curb her vegetable cravings. She grabbed a bottle of water, then thought a moment before grabbing another. Then she paid for them at the counter. She held her breath as she left the store, her eyes darting around the parking lot. To her relief, it appeared Jefferson had left. She carried her bag of treasures to her home behind the restaurant, preparing her bed so that she had a nice place to sit and enjoy her feast. Once she was settled, she opened the lid to the chicken and was greeted by its fragrant steam. Nothing had ever smelled better. She pulled off a bit of the breast and bit into it, the juice from the meat exploding in her mouth and dribbling down her chin. She tore into the chicken, unable to eat fast enough. It felt like she could breathe again. She added in bites of salad in between mouthfuls of chicken, and then began on the French bread. She sipped small bits of water to wash it all down, careful not to drink too much so that it wouldn't fill her up.

Her stomach swelled when she finally finished, and she stretched back, happy and satiated. Looking up, she noticed the old man under the tree watching her.

"Come here," she said, beckoning him with a wave of her hand. He only scooted further away. "Please," she said. "I have all this food, and I can't eat another bite. Will you help me by taking the rest of it?" He remained under the tree, but she could see the hint of interest on his face, even under the dim light of the streetlamps. "Come on, sir," she coaxed him. "It's much better than the food you've been getting out of there," she added, waving her hand toward the dumpster.

The man sighed, then stood. He scooted down the embankment then shuffled to where she was sitting. Then he squatted down a safe distance away from her. Maddie pushed the food toward him, and placed a bottle of water in his hand.

"Go ahead," she prompted, nodding toward the food. He reached forward, continuing to watch her as he tore piece after piece from the chicken and placed them in his mouth. He had no teeth, Maddie realized, but still managed to chew the food and swallow it, grabbing for more after each bite. Then he opened the bottle of water and sipped from it. He took a deep breath and let it out, relaxing from his squat into a sitting position.

"Not like us," he muttered, once he had eaten a good amount. He looked her over, and then snorted.

"What do you mean?" she asked. "Of course I like you. I'm giving you food, right?"

"No," he said, frustration apparent in the word. "You. Different. Won't be here long. Not like us." He pointed to her belly. "You need home. Not this." Then he stood. He gave her a bow and a small smile, then shuffled back to his place under the tree.

Maddie picked up the naked chicken and other remnants of their curbside banquet and tossed them in the garbage can. She digested the man's words as the meal sat heavy in her stomach. She hoped he was right. She couldn't bear the thought of growing old like this. More than that, she couldn't imagine what it would be like to raise her child here. If her math was correct, she only had four more months until the baby was born. Whatever happened after that, Maddie couldn't bear to imagine. She didn't know what she was going to do once the baby came, or even how it would happen. All she knew was that there was no way her baby could survive a life like this. Something had to happen, and fast. She hoped the man's words were more of a prophecy. She hoped she wouldn't be homeless for long.

Jill

- Twenty -
Starting Small

"I want to do something, Michael," Jill said, setting her fork down on the side of her plate. Ever since meeting Oliver the week before, she hadn't been able to get him, and even Albert, out of her mind. It had all started with Maddie, but her eyes were now opened to the plight of the many more out there who had far less than everyone else, and were treated as the scum of society. She was so consumed by this, that even eating dinner in restaurant with her husband seemed awfully frivolous. She couldn't help feeling guilty about the amount of money they were spending on a mere meal when there were people out there starving.

"What do you have in mind?" Michael asked. Jill gave him a grateful smile. She knew he was still treating her with kid gloves, afraid of what new scheme she was trying to rope him into. But it meant a lot to her that he was actually willing to listen to her first.

"I don't know," she admitted. "But something." He gave her a quizzical look.

"Like what?" he prompted her.

"I mean, don't you ever feel like we could be doing more for others? Like, maybe we're not doing enough?" she asked.

"I don't know," Michael said. "I mean, I never really thought about it. But I guess, yeah, we could always do more."

"So what should we do?"

"I don't know, Jill," Michael sighed. "Maybe donate money or something? Or we could bag groceries at the food bank? I mean, it's not like we have loads of time. You're talking about getting a job, and I already work full-time. When is there time for us?"

"We have lots of time for us," Jill pointed out. "I feel like we do the same thing every night." She caught the look on his face. "Not that it's a bad thing," she quickly added. "I just feel like the time we're spending just sitting around could be spent better, like helping those who don't have all the comforts and luxuries we have."

"I guess," Michael said, hesitancy still on his face. "Don't get me wrong, I want to help others, too. But it's hard to know what I'm agreeing to if I don't know what's going on in your mind." He gave Jill a half smile, and took her hand. "Your heart is in the right place. I want to support you. But I guess I need more information before I agree for us to commit. What if you went to one of the local churches or the homeless shelter and ask what their biggest needs are? Or you could hold a clothing or diaper drive, or even a canned food drive. Get out there and get information, but not just from me. I mean, you could even sit down with that homeless guy and ask him what he thinks would be helpful."

"You mean Oliver?" Jill asked.

"Yeah, why not? I mean, he would know more than anyone what would make his situation more comfortable," Michael said.

"This is true," Jill said. She picked up her fork and took another bite, a million possibilities rolling through her head regarding how she could help. Maybe bring the community together to build an apartment complex for the homeless, or a place that guaranteed work for those willing to lift a hand for money, or even creating a store for donations where those in need could get them for free.

But the next day when she inquired about needs at the local shelter, she was urged to try a different direction.

"Start small," the woman on the phone said. She had told Jill her name, something like Mary Isaac. And when Jill gave her a shy report on what she hoped to accomplish, Mary gently encouraged smaller, easier ways to help.

"There are a lot of people who want to give to those in need, and we couldn't run our program without them," Mary told her. "Currently, we have a need for volunteer drivers to help deliver meals or take clients to their various appointments. Or you could help out in the kitchen, either cooking or putting together food boxes, or even just washing dishes or helping to load the trucks."

Jill told her she'd think about it, and thanked her for her time. But when she got off the phone, she crossed that option off the list. She didn't want to volunteer for another program. She wanted to create a program of her own to help those in need.

Next she mulled over calling a church. But she didn't even know where to start. She and Michael were not churchgoers in the least, not even for holidays. She was afraid that if she called a church to find out how she could help, the pastor would discover she didn't go to church and somehow guilt her into attending service. That nixed that idea.

Frustrated, Jill got in the car and started driving. She headed to the parking lot of Food Mart. But this time, instead of looking for Maddie, she sought out Oliver. He wasn't hard to find. He was in front of the grocery store, once again surrounded by a small group of people as he gave one of his mini performances.

"Can we talk?" Jill asked, once he was done. He grinned at her and patted the seat next to him.

"What's shaking?" he asked. "Did you bring me one of your infamous PB and Js?" Jill groaned, shaking her head.

"I didn't even think about it," she admitted. "I'm sorry, I'll bring one next time. Can I get you anything else?"

"Nah," he grinned. "I already ate. I actually got a secret paying gig from the store here. They give me $20 and three square meals if I'll hang out here during the day. They figure it will keep the other homeless people from sitting here, driving away business. I get to keep all the money thrown in my hat, and I'm full all day long. Before long, I might have enough to buy the whole store." He winked as she chuckled. "So what's on your mind?"

"Well, I have this idea rolling around in my head, but I don't know how to make it happen," Jill began. She suddenly felt shy, her ears going hot as she fiddled with her hands. "I just got to thinking about all the stuff you told me last week, how people have this specific view of the homeless, and don't know how to give without passing judgment or conditions. I want a way to help you, and other people like you. But I also want to help bridge that gap between the needy and those who could actually make a difference."

"Okay…" he said. "So what was your idea?"

"That's where you come in. I don't know." She looked at him, feeling really stupid. "I'm sorry, this is dumb. Just forget it."

"Now hold on there, ma'am. It's never dumb to want to help others. You just have to remember, while you might want to give, you may not get the reaction you're expecting. You remember Albert and the sandwich, right?"

"Yeah, I remember," she said. It still stung, even though she tried to brush it off.

"Now multiply that by ten, twenty, even fifty more, depending on how big your plan is aiming to be. Can you handle it if you go out of your way to do something nice only to have it shot down by the very people you're trying to help?" he asked. Jill looked at her hands again, then back to him.

"That's why I'm coming to you," she said. "I want to *know* what you need, what the other men in this lot need, and what any other person who doesn't have a home might need. I don't want to put myself out there and supply what

I *think* you need. I want to be able to make a difference for you and people like you on *your* terms."

"Well, I don't need anything," Oliver said, sitting back against the wall with a grin. He gestured all around them. "I have the sky as my ceiling, the wind as my walls, and nature as my soundtrack. No one tells me what to do or who to be. I'm free, and I wouldn't want it any other way."

"But does everyone feel that way?" Jill asked.

"No, not everyone. But many of us do. There's an old man behind the restaurant who doesn't trust anyone or anything. I could never see him get anywhere near a shelter. I don't know what happened to that guy, but ain't nobody able to get near him. And then there's Albert over there. I know he'd love to stay in the shelter. But they don't allow dogs in there. And if Rusty can't go, then neither will Al. As for your girl? I don't know why she won't sleep there. Maybe she just doesn't know about it or something. But in her condition, a warm place to sleep and a soft mattress would be much better than sleeping in a parking lot."

"So maybe there needs to be a place where people can get information," Jill mused. "Like where they can go to escape the cold, maybe how they can get medical care, or even where to find low-cost food."

"Now you're thinking," Oliver said. "How about haircuts? I could definitely use one of those." He lifted his hat to show off his mop of hair before putting it back on.

"What else?" Jill asked, reaching into her purse for a pad of paper.

"Well, definitely some of those sandwiches you make so well."

"Seriously, Oliver? I can make other things much better than peanut butter and jelly," she said.

"I'm sure you can. But those happen to be a personal favorite of mine." He nodded at her list. "Write it down." She did, with a laugh.

Together, the two of them hashed out a plan that would both help, and be easy to implement. All Jill had to do was get enough people to back up their plan. She left Oliver that afternoon, driving home with her head brimming with ideas. As soon as she got home, she thumbed through her contacts, making a list of everyone she knew who might want to help. She drafted an email that detailed her plan and what she hoped they'd accomplish, leaving the invitation open for further ideas should anyone have any. Then she picked up the phone and began dialing people one by one.

"Lucy? Hey, I have a favor to ask of you, and it's kind of huge. Do you have a moment?"

Maddie

~ Twenty-one ~
Reasons to Forget

The days were cooling, and the nights were close to unbearable. Maddie had thought it was cold when she first hit the streets in July. Now that it was October, the wind turned from a cool breeze to, at times, an icy blast impossible to escape. The old man who shared her corner of the parking lot seemed to be surviving it, so Maddie was determined she would, too. Still she worried more and more about what would happen once the baby was born.

Morning was hitting the parking lot, the sun breaking through the patchy fog to reach Maddie where she slept. Her body, while used to the hard pavement, was sore from the work she'd been doing lately. She'd been so proficient with her work at the Winstons' that sometimes there just wasn't enough stuff to do. And still, Mr. Winston sent Jefferson to pick her up every weekday. At first she had sat in the house, taking her time on certain chores so that it didn't appear she was done. But Mr. Winston had caught on quick. Rather than send her home, he had seated her at the sorting table with a few of the men to go through the grapes and pick out the bad ones. When harvest came to a close, he found other odd jobs for her. Always it required her to sit instead of stand. But still, it didn't stop the strain in her back or the stiffness in her neck.

Maddie grabbed the oversized dress from beside her makeshift bed and slipped it over her head. She'd been lucky to find a whole bag full of maternity clothes a few months before, giving her something to wear as her body expanded. The baby nudged at her belly as she moved, and Maddie groaned at the discomfort. The baby was getting big, and so was she. When she was standing, she couldn't even see the tips of her toes. And getting up and down from a seated position was getting harder and harder—especially from the asphalt. Maddie struggled to get a knee up under her, using it to hold her weight as she tried to hoist herself up. No matter how hard she tried this time, however, her sore muscles wouldn't cooperate.

"I help," the old man said, at her side in an instant. He grabbed her arm and put it on his shoulder, letting her use him for leverage while he pulled at her. With their joint effort, she was able to stand. She gave him a grateful, if not embarrassed, smile.

"Thank you," she said to him. She still didn't know his name, and he didn't seem to remember hers. But it didn't seem to matter. Over the months, they'd grown accustomed to being roommates in their unconventional home, looking out for each other like family. In some ways, he felt like both her father and her child. He looked at her now, a sadness in his smile. He reached forward and patted her arm.

"You find home now. Don't come back," he said. She smiled. He always said that. She wished she could make it happen.

"I'll try," she said, taking his hand and squeezing it. She grabbed her bag, something she had started carrying months before. It held the baby blanket the woman had given her, and all of her money—all $600 of it—in a jar. Sometimes when the weather was especially cool, or the ground felt more than hard, Maddie had felt tempted to use the money to seek out a motel room for the night. She was too scared to stay in a shelter, afraid they would assume she was a runaway and arrest her. But at a hotel, she could enjoy a night of sleeping in a real bed with a real pillow. But each time she thought about it, she also thought of the baby. A night at a motel would eat up too much of what she had saved so far. That money was meant for raising her baby. Spending it on her own comfort would be a frivolous expense.

Maddie waved goodbye to the old man, then walked to the front of the store to wait for Jefferson to pick her up. He came only a few minutes later.

"Where to, Miss?" he asked with a wink when she got in. She laughed, knowing he was aware of the same dress she wore every day, and the way her hair refused to stay flat even when she pulled it back in a ponytail.

"How about Spain, sir?" she asked. "Or maybe the south of France."

"Why stop there? A trip around the world, as the lady ordered," he said in a deep voice, pulling the car away from the curb.

Maddie watched out the window as they drove, never growing tired of the rolling hills with golden vines. The glow from the sunrise only added to the orange and yellow colors among the fields. New Mexico was starting to feel like a faraway place. California was her home now, one way or another.

They pulled up to the house, and Jefferson opened her door for her.

"Thank you, Jefferson," she said, giving him a nod.

"My pleasure, Maddie," he said, his smile warm as he tipped his hat and closed the door.

Maddie walked up the steps and let herself in. It still felt odd to do that—to enter someone else's home without knocking first. But Mr. Winston had insisted on it, telling her that it would be less of a strain on Mrs. Winston if she didn't have to get up and answer the door. And so she did.

Mrs. Winston was sitting at the table, looking out the window when Maddie walked in. She didn't look in Maddie's direction when she entered. Looking closer, Maddie could see that the woman was deep in thought. She put the tea water on and started washing the dishes while it heated up. When the whistle blew, she grabbed a cup and a tea bag, pouring the steaming water to create a fragrant herbal brew.

"Here you go, Mrs. Winston," she said, placing the cup in front of her before adding in two sugar cubes, just the way the old woman liked it. Mrs. Winston looked up. Her eyes were watery, but she smiled as if they weren't. She took Maddie's hand and patted it.

"You're such a good girl," she said. "If only my own daughter were like you." The sad smile returned to her face, and she looked out the window once again.

Mrs. Winston had mentioned her daughter to Maddie on several occasions. But lately, it seemed this mysterious girl haunted the old woman's mind. In the past week, not a day had passed when she didn't say something about her daughter. However, Maddie had never seen any family pictures on the walls. The only people who came to visit the Winstons were a few of their friends or people who came to talk business with Mr. Winston.

She had never asked the couple about their family or any of their personal history. It had always felt too intrusive. Plus, any questions she asked only invited questions about her own life—a life she wanted to leave far behind her.

But on this day, her curiosity got the better of her. Mrs. Winston looked so sad, so troubled. If she had at least a hint as to why, maybe she could help.

"When will your daughter come to visit, Mrs. Winston?" she asked. A pained look crossed the older woman's face, and Maddie regretted the question immediately.

"I...I...I don't know," the woman said. She looked around the room, confusion washing over her face. "I'm not sure where she went." The way her expression fell as she said it, Maddie couldn't help but absorb some of her sadness. She touched Mrs. Winston's arm, but the woman moved away. "I think I need to go lie down," she said. She looked lost as she stood, and Maddie followed close behind to make sure she made it to her room all right.

When her bedroom door had closed, Maddie went back downstairs to start on her list of chores. But all she could see was the sadness in Mrs. Winston's face. She had to know why the woman was so troubled. Something had happened, she knew it. Against her better judgment, she left the kitchen and sought out Mr. Winston. She found him in his office, studying papers that lay across his desk, just as he often did in the afternoons. He looked up when she knocked lightly on the open door.

"How can I be of service to you, Maddie, dear?" he asked. She smiled at the familiarity he used with her name, but then furrowed her brow at the questions she hoped he would answer.

"Mr. Winston, I know it's none of my business. But Mrs. Winston keeps mentioning a daughter. And yet, I never see any of your family coming to visit." She was going to keep going, but noticed that Mr. Winston's expression had fallen, silencing any further questions she had for him. He took his glasses off and rubbed at the space between his eyes before putting them back on. He then motioned for her to come further into the room.

"Close the door behind you," he said, and she did. She then sat in the leather chair that faced his desk, running her hands over the smooth red material.

"I'm sorry, Mr. Winston. I shouldn't have asked. It's none of my business," she said.

"No, it's okay. Mrs. Winston hasn't been herself this past week, and I think she's fixated her mind on our daughter. It's probably best if you know." He took in a deep breath and looked at the ceiling, letting it out in a heavy sigh.

Maddie stayed still, even though the ache in her back was worsening. The chair was too hard against her tightened muscles. But she refrained from fidgeting in case it made Mr. Winston change his mind.

"We were young when we got married," he began. "But when you know, you know. And I wasn't going to let anything come between me and marrying Viola." Maddie's eyes widened at Mr. Winston's casual use of his wife's first name. It was the first time she had ever heard it. "It wasn't long after that when she got pregnant and we welcomed home a beautiful baby girl. We named her Eleanor, but she was forever known as Ellie. She had the most beguiling smile and bouncing blonde curls one ever did see, and she could charm even the most stubborn person into doing her bidding. She was our only child, and we made sure she had the best of everything. When Ellie was still a baby, I bought this piece of land from an aging farmer, and I learned all I could about vineyards and winemaking. We were fortunate to be able to build our wealth substantially over the years. As a result, Ellie was given everything we never had growing up." He stopped, and Maddie couldn't miss the catch in his throat. He removed his glasses again and squeezed between his eyes, as if the pain could take away whatever it was he was about to tell her.

"I'm sorry, Mr. Winston," Maddie said. She rose from the chair, her back aching even more with the movement. "I didn't mean to pry. I should go."

"No, don't go. Let me finish," he pleaded. She had never seen him this way. Usually Mr. Winston was either cheerful or stern, and always strong in his demeanor. Now, he seemed helpless, almost frail. Maddie sat back in the chair, fighting a grimace as the pain settled back into her lower back.

"When Ellie was about your age, she fell in love with a boy that Viola and I had a hard time liking," Mr. Winston continued. "We didn't know him very well, but what we did know of him wasn't very good. We just couldn't find it in ourselves to approve of him. When Ellie started to date him, she began acting differently. She wasn't the girl we had raised her to be. At night she would sneak out to see this boy against our will. Sometimes she would disappear for days at a time. She no longer showed any care for her mother or me. Eventually she threw it in our faces that she was pregnant, and was leaving forever. In her mind, her mother and I were the enemy. She was convinced that we oppressed her and prevented her from being who she really was. Perhaps we did, I don't know. We only wanted the best for her. But maybe we were too hard on her, pushing her too much..." He paused to take a few deep breaths, and ran his hands through his thin hair. He looked at Maddie and continued. "She left, and we didn't hear from her for months." Mr. Winston stood from the desk and went to his window, looking outside at the vibrant vineyards that lined the hillside behind the house. Maddie stayed where she was, waiting for him to finish.

"It was late one night when Mrs. Winston and I heard something out in the workshop. I thought it was an animal or something. I grabbed my rifle, only meaning to scare it away. I don't know why I didn't grab a shoe, or a rock, or something I could have just thrown. For some reason, it was the rifle that found my hands first. But when I came upon the workshop, I was glad I had it. I heard a man's voice order me to drop the gun. In the dark I could see two figures, and one of them was coming at me. I fired two shots without thinking. I had been afraid they were going to come in the house for Viola. One of the thieves dropped to the ground, the other made it out the window and drove off. And when I turned on the light…" Mr. Winston stopped, stifling a cry into his fist as he continued to stare out the window. "When I turned on the light, it was Ellie. She had died instantly. Worse, she had been telling the truth about her pregnancy…" Mr. Winston's voice shook, his eyes filling with tears. He left the window and sat back down, clearing his throat a few times to try and compose himself. "I reckon they were trying to steal a few things for money when I caught them. They may have been doing it for months, judging by the things I thought I'd misplaced during the time Ellie had been gone. I had to tell Viola what had happened, and as you can imagine, she was more than distraught. When Ellie had left the first time, Viola had blamed herself. Now she wasn't sure what to think. It took a toll on our marriage, on our well-being, on what we thought we knew about life. Of course, the investigation cleared the death as an accident. But that didn't lessen our guilt and shame. We couldn't talk to anyone about what had happened. What would they think?" He looked at Maddie then, and she realized how significant this was that he was telling her. Had he never told anyone else? Why was he telling her this now?

"You know that Mrs. Winston is not herself these later years. In the short amount of time you've known us, I know you see this about my wife," he said, to which Maddie nodded. "She has been slowly losing her memory. As of late, she's been fixating on the memory of Ellie, but she's remembering things about her that never really happened. It's like her memory is adding the parts in where Ellie's life ended, giving her a second chance at knowing her daughter. And I don't know where to let it lie and where to correct her." He sighed, giving Maddie a pointed look. "This is why she chose you," he said. "We weren't even looking for a worker that day. We were just going for a drive, and stopped at the store. But when we saw you, both of us couldn't turn away. You reminded us of her then, and you still remind us of her. You have her same spirit—an independent teen way beyond your years. And yet, you possess a wisdom about you that we never really got to see in Ellie. In a way, you're like the prodigal daughter returned, as if you are her coming back to us after all this time."

Maddie shifted uncomfortably in her chair, her cheeks feeling flush at the comparison. "But Mr. Winston, I'm not your daughter." He gave her a tired smile, his eyes kind as he nodded.

"I know, dear," he said. "And thank goodness for that, because you are a good girl with a good head on your shoulders. Lord only knows how we would have ruined you had we been the ones who raised you." He gave a soft laugh, but Maddie couldn't help but notice the darkness in his words. "I've made peace with what happened, at least as much peace as I ever will. And Viola, she manages the only way she knows how—by forgetting. But underneath, I know she feels the same way I do, that no amount of regret is going to bring Ellie back. Still, when we saw you that first morning, a tiny, determined little thing waiting in the early hours of the morning for work, we couldn't help but see some of our daughter. There was no chance of us being able to turn away."

Maddie took in a deep breath, the dull pain in her back so intense she felt nauseous. Something about what Mr. Winston said struck her. She wasn't sure if she felt comforted or troubled by what they saw in her. Part of her understood. But the talk of their troubled relationship with their daughter brought on thoughts of her own parents. Images of her mom and dad flashed through her mind, and the room felt like it was closing in on her. She stood up quick, unable to suppress the cry that escaped her lips at the sharp pain in her lower abdomen. She winced, doing her best to compose herself.

"Are you okay?" Mr. Winston asked, standing up quick. Maddie masked the pain with a smile, and she nodded.

"Yes, I'm fine. But I think I need a little air. Could you give me a few moments?" She turned toward the door and grasped the handle.

"Are you sure?" he asked. "I can drive you home if you'd like." Maddie shook her head no. She could feel the panic welling up inside of her. She needed to get out.

"I'm fine," she repeated. "I just need some air." She opened the door and closed it behind her. The pain in her belly was spreading across her abdomen, taking her breath away. She grabbed her bag off the hook, and then opened the front door, nearly falling down the steps to the driveway. The ache in her back was radiating down her legs, the pressure inside of her mounting. She needed to find a place where she could just lay down and not have anyone look at her. She'd be fine if she could just lay down.

The fields of vines were calling to her. She veered to her left and started toward the hillside. Pausing at the edge, she looked behind her to see if anyone was following her. They weren't. She turned back to the vines, stepping over the threshold and disappearing within the lined corridors of golden yellow leaves.

Maddie

-Twenty-two -
The Road to Hope

Unable to go any further, Maddie collapsed on the dirt, thick within the vine covered hill. From where she was, she couldn't see the house. The pain shot through her like lightning, each jolt more severe than the last, and she took turns curling up into a fetal position and stretching out long. It didn't matter which way she moved, the pain seized her, crippling her with each shocking cramp.

The baby was coming. The doctor had told her it wouldn't be until November. It was too early.

Maddie tried to get up again. She didn't know why she had come so far into the hill, why she felt the need to hide away from everyone else. Something about Mr. Winston's story had bothered her, or maybe it was just the beginning labor pains. She wasn't sure. She had just felt the need to get away. Perhaps it was the shame of being like Ellie, disappointing her parents in being something they didn't want her to be. Maybe it was understanding the look of pain on Mrs. Winston's face, wondering if her mother carried the same regretful look. Maybe it was just the pain and the feelings of nausea that made her want to get away from everyone and everything.

Now she wished someone was there to help her.

A sharp contraction ripped through her, and she groaned in agony. She fought the urge to cry out, unwilling to submit to the fire inside. She deserved this. Of every wrong thing she had done in her life, this was her penance. She felt a gush of water flow between her legs, wetting the earth beneath her, a small sense of relief washing over her. It didn't last long. The pain returned, grabbing hold of her without letting go. This time she couldn't hold back, her scream echoing through the hillside, scattering the birds who flocked in the trees behind her. The pain subsided, and she lay panting, clawing at the ground as if she might be hurled into space if she didn't.

"Oh God," she moaned. "Please help me." It was the closest she'd ever come to praying. Even in her darkest moments, she had never turned to God. That was her mom's deal, not hers. Besides, it wasn't like God was there when she grew up, when she got pregnant, when her parents kicked her out, or when she was abandoned in a Petaluma parking lot. But there she was, laying helpless in a field of vines, pleading with a force she wasn't sure even existed. "Please God, help me," she whimpered. "Help me….help me….help me…."

Her anguish ebbed, and she became aware of thick footsteps tromping through the weeds. A brown face peeked through the leaves, his olive green eyes widening when he caught sight of Maddie laying on the ground. He was young, maybe fourteen, probably the son of one of the workers.

"Chica," he breathed, frozen where he stood. Maddie looked up at him, gripping the earth, terror in her eyes.

"Ayuda me," she whispered in halting Spanish, hoping he knew what to do. He started to turn away from her. "Wait," she pleaded. She could feel the pressure, wanting to push. She lost all words, the fire in her groin and abdomen burning her inside out. "Don't leave me," she managed to get out. The pain surged through her, and she groaned somewhere deep in her belly, the sound of her voice foreign to her ears. The boy knelt at Maddie's knees. She could see tears filling his wide eyes. He was scared. Well, she was, too. The pain subsided for a moment, and she breathed, the sweat pouring off her forehead and into her eyes. He reached forward, taking his sleeve and wiping her forehead. She gave him a grateful smile.

"We're going to do this together," she told him, bracing herself for the next contraction. She knew he didn't understand her, but it didn't matter. He was there. She wasn't alone. "You and me, okay?" she whispered.

"You. Me. Okay," the boy said. He took a deep breath and let it out, a determined look taking over the fear in his eyes. With trembling hands, he took off his sweatshirt and laid it on the ground between her legs. Then he reached down, and she saw his lip quiver for a moment. He touched her underpants, now soaked through. "Okay?" he asked. She nodded. He carefully slid her underwear off as she lifted her hips. It was too late for modesty. "Okay," he whispered. Maddie felt the next agonizing wave surging through her, and the pressure mounting against her groin. She bore down with the pain, a low guttural moan escaping from her mouth as she pushed with everything she had. "Es okay, es okay," the boy repeated over and over. He held her legs open, his face focused as he prepared himself. "Es okay, es okay."

Maddie could feel the pressure deepening, a flash of electricity convulsing through her as she kept pushing. She paused to breathe, crying against the pain that enflamed her back and twisted her insides. She wanted to stop. It hurt too much. Maybe the earth would just swallow her whole. She looked up and caught the boy's eyes, focusing on the light green of his iris. The sudden connection grounded her, speaking more than their language barrier allowed them to do with words. He gave her a slow nod, his eyes never breaking from hers. She mirrored his solemn face, her cries subsiding as she contained herself, remembering why she was here. She couldn't give up.

"Uno," the boy said, keeping his eyes locked with hers. "Dos," he counted, and she dug her hands around the weeds beside her. "Ahora!" he demanded, and she closed her eyes and pushed, breathing out in a heavy groan as she used every bit of strength she had. The boy murmured words she couldn't quite make out, words she didn't understand. But she focused on them to remove herself from the fire within her. She felt the baby crowning. The pain intensified, searing through her, but she kept with it. The boy leaned forward as she pushed, and he caught the baby as it came out. She could hear its thick cries as she collapsed against the ground.

"Es un niña," the boy told her. She smiled. A girl. She laid back on the dirt in exhaustion as he placed the crying baby in the sweatshirt. Then he handed the baby to Maddie and smiled. She could see relief on his face.

"I get help," he said in broken English, backing away. He then disappeared into the vines, his footsteps pounding the earth as he ran.

Maddie looked down at the little girl in her arms. She had a mass of black matted hair on her head, her skin red and blotchy from the trauma of being born. Her eyes blinked, heavy with fatigue. Maddie watched as she fought to keep them open. She had stopped crying and her eyes darted around, her gaze occasionally landing on her mother. Maddie stared at the baby's tiny rosebud mouth, watching as the tiny girl pursed her lips, opening and closing them. Her body seemed so delicate, lost in the giant sweatshirt she was wrapped in.

"Hope," Maddie said, trying the name out on her. She hadn't thought of a name in all her pregnancy, afraid to make it more real than it already was. But now, she knew there was no other name that would do. "Hope," she said again, smiling into the tiny face. She hadn't had much hope lately. Her whole world had shattered when she was thrown from her parents' house. She had grown up fast when she moved to an unfamiliar state. She had learned to fend for herself when Jordan left her at the curb. And now, she was surviving by just a string of hope left.

Maddie peered into her daughter's face, hoping she could give her the life she didn't have. She hoped her daughter would never feel the pain of loss and poverty, two companions that had stayed with her the last several months.

A cold wind rustled through the leaves, passing through the vines and over Maddie. She shivered. She looked around her, coming to her senses about where she was, what she was doing. How was she going to take care of this child? She had hardly been able to take care of herself from the moment she found herself on her own. It was by grace that she had survived this long, and that the Winstons had found her. If they had passed her by, she might have died. Without them, she was nothing. Even now, she had no means to provide for a baby. She had no home. She barely had any money. If the Winstons decided they didn't need her anymore, she would be right back where she started. Where was Hope going to sleep—near the trash can with her?

Looking down at her daughter, now asleep in her arms, Maddie realized she already loved her more than anything in the whole world. Tears sprang to her eyes as she felt her heart swell in her chest. It seemed incredible to Maddie that this tiny being could entice such strong feelings of protectiveness within her. She knew she'd do anything to ensure Hope didn't suffer the life Maddie had been living the past several months. If it were asked of her, Maddie knew she would die for this little girl. It made her heart ache, knowing her own mother had once looked down on her, feeling the same intense feelings over her. Did her mother still think of her? Was she thinking of her now?

Maddie laid Hope on the ground, the sweatshirt still wrapped around her. Carefully, she unfolded the fabric, revealing Hope's tiny body still stained with blood. Maddie's bag lay beside her, and she pulled it closer. From inside she took out the bottle of water and the patchwork quilt, laying the blanket on the ground next to them. With the water, she wet a clean corner of the sweatshirt and smoothed it over Hope's body. She wet her hands, touching her daughter's soft skin. The baby moved in her sleep, wrinkling her face at the shock of cool water. She opened her mouth, mewing her delicate cries into the wind. Maddie finished cleaning her, shushing her as she moved, then wrapped her in the clean quilt.

"There now," she whispered, the baby quieting as she came close to her mother's skin. Maddie realized she might be hungry, unsure if she even knew how to feed her. She bared her breast, bringing the baby closer, moving until the baby caught her scent. It took a little effort, but she eventually figured it out, latching on and beginning to drink.

Maddie watched her nursing daughter, the dread inside her intensifying as she racked her brain to figure out what she was going to do. She didn't even have clothes for her, not even diapers. She had nothing to offer her at all except for love—and that wasn't going to keep her alive. She was out of options. She swore she'd never let her daughter be homeless. She swore she'd never let her experience poverty like this.

She knew there was no other choice.

Jill

~ Twenty-three ~
Maddie's Mission

Jill took a deep breath, looking at her reflection in the mirror above her dresser. She had come a long way in the last six months. She glanced down at the small picture frame in the corner of the dresser top. Picking it up, she looked into Toby's face that filled the frame, his captured smile radiant as he waited for her to put down the camera and pick him up. Sometimes it felt like it had been years since she held him. Other times, only days. Always, she ached to be able to wrap him in her arms again.

"Today's the big day, kiddo," she said to the picture. She wondered sometimes if he heard her from wherever he was. She liked to think he did.

She picked her purse up, unable to resist looking inside. Between her wallet and her cell phone was a wrapped present. She pulled it out, knowing what lay inside. She smiled, enjoying the secret only she knew. It would have to wait a little while longer, though. When she heard Michael's footsteps down the hall, she dropped the gift box back in her purse and shut it tight.

"Are you ready?" he asked from the doorway. She looked at him, smiling at his appearance. He wore the same t-shirt she did, the words "Maddie's Mission" emblazoned across the back. After months of planning, it was finally happening.

Michael drove to the parking lot, parking near the large canvas tent that had already been set up.

"Will this work okay?" her friend, Paula, asked. "I got it donated from a rental company looking to upgrade."

"It's perfect!" Jill exclaimed. She helped Michael carry boxes of food, placing them at one of the tables. She had made several different varieties of cookies and hundreds of sandwiches, including Oliver's favorites—peanut butter and jelly. Already on the table were bottled waters and bags of chips, as well as a stack of paper lunch bags. She felt a tap on her shoulder, and turned to find Sue, a woman she had connected with through one of the local churches.

"Jill, I set up the baby area in the corner over there," Sue said, pointing to the other side of the tent. Jill looked to where she was pointing, and smiled, even as her eyes watered. A large banner hung over a play area, "The Toby Project" in large, colorful letters across it. Below it there were several play structures perfect for toddlers to climb on, with toys stacked neatly in boxes beside them. Jill chuckled, remembering how Toby used to pull everything he owned out of the boxes. She wondered how long the neatly stacked boxes would last.

"I placed the family donation area next to The Toby Project," Sue told her.

"Oh good," Jill said. "I have a few items in my car I wanted to drop off."

She left the tented area to grab a few bags off her backseat. She had found boxes of clothes Toby had outgrown in their garage, forgotten about until just recently. This time she didn't even look through them. She didn't have to. Someone else needed them much more than she did.

She closed the door and turned around, pausing to lean against her car as she surveyed the whole area. The food table and The Toby Project stood as bookends to the services they were providing for low-income and homeless families. In between them was a station where people could get free haircuts, a table with information on shelters, housing and medical help, a booth to help people fill out job applications and find out about childcare, and boxes filled with more donated clothing and items. About two dozen volunteers moved from table to table, working to get everything done in time. Many of them she hadn't even known until just recently. She had started with her friends, who then asked their friends, leading to a domino effect of people who jumped at the chance to do something for the less fortunate in their area. From hanging posters, to an ad in the newspaper, to everything that stood before her in the parking lot now…it was all from people who wanted to give up a bit of their time for those in need.

"Come on, Jill!" one of the ladies called out to her with a grin and a wave. Jill beamed, taking the bag of donations to The Toby Project before joining the team of volunteers.

"I think they need a pep talk from their fearless leader," Michael said as they huddled together. Jill felt her ears grow hot. She wasn't keen on public speaking. But when she looked around at the group of people smiling at her, waiting for her words, she saw a group of friends. And she smiled back at them, relaxing into herself as she took her husband's hand, and then the hand of the person next to her. Everyone else followed suit until all hands were held in the circle.

"Six months ago, my whole entire world was turned upside down," Jill began. Her eyes filled with tears, but she smiled through them, determined to be brave and say everything she needed to say without breaking down. "My son died. I didn't even know that was possible, that children could die. I mean, you hear about it all the time. And you feel bad for those it happens to. But it seems impossible for something so terrible like that to happen to you until *it happens to you*. So when my son died, in a way, I died, too. I stopped existing. I was so wrapped up in my grief I could barely breathe. And I couldn't see that other people in this world were suffering at the very same time. It wasn't until a young girl named Maddie opened my eyes." Jill looked up at her husband and smiled, wiggling her fingers in his hand—the same fingers that had been cooped up in a cast just a few weeks earlier. "Now, I doubt Maddie even realizes she changed my life. She doesn't know me, and I don't really know her. But somehow she still showed me that hardships exist all around us, and people are surviving, even when they're hurting. Because of her, I have met some of the most amazing people; some who have far less than any of us could imagine, and some of them with the most compassionate hearts I have ever known....people like you." She grinned at the crowd around her as they murmured words of encouragement. "None of this could have happened without your help. Maddie's Mission began as an idea. But it's all of you who made it happen. So thank you." She took a deep breath, raising the hands she was holding. Everyone else followed suit so that the circle was bursting like a sunbeam. "Are you ready?" she asked.

"Ready!" the volunteers shouted. Jill grinned.

"All right, let's do this then!"

They all broke apart and went to their stations. Already a small crowd was forming, mostly out of curiosity about the tent at the end of the parking lot. More and more people trickled over, both those in need and those wondering what they could do to help with future events. Jill stayed in the center of the crowd, answering all questions and coordinating volunteer efforts. She grinned when she saw Oliver sitting in one of the chairs at the haircutting booth, going from shaggy long hair to something more clean-cut. She noticed he kept the beard, though.

"Like the 'do?" he asked her about ten minutes later, sidling up to her as soon as there was a lull in the crowd.

"I love it!" she said. "You better watch out, Oliver, you almost look handsome."

"Damn these devilish good looks!" he said, wrinkling his nose and stroking his beard. Jill laughed, patting her friend's free hand.

"Oliver, when are you going to accept a little help from Michael and me and let us get you an apartment," she asked him, her facing turning serious.

"You mean, joining the workforce and putting on a suit and tie?" he asked. "Never. I'm quite happy here." He kicked back and gave his guitar a quick strum to push his point home. "Plus, now you're about to bring all this great food. Why should I leave?" he asked, giving her a wink. "Speaking of food…"

She was one step ahead of him, placing a peanut butter and jelly sandwich in his hands.

"We've got to stop meeting like this," he whispered, taking a bite of the sandwich with a wink. She laughed. Then she looked around.

"Hey, how's Albert doing?" she asked. She hadn't seen him at the tent all day long, not that she expected it. Still, she worried about him. It had been a month since Rusty had passed away. Ever since, the old man had been even less responsive than before.

"Oh, you know Albert. Some days he's good, most days he's not. It's hard to say what's normal and what isn't. I'd worry about him, except I never really liked the guy much, anyway." Even saying that, Jill didn't miss the concerned look on his face. She looked across the parking lot, seeing the old man slouched in his usual spot in front of the pharmacy. His head was down, but she could see him move as he looked up every few minutes. She turned back to Oliver and gave him a reassuring smile.

"I'll check on him before we pack it in," she told him. "And even if he refuses, I'll bring him a lunch bag of food. You never know, today night be the day."

"Never know," Oliver agreed, winking at her before getting up and walking away, strumming his guitar as he left.

"Jill!"

Jill turned to see who was calling her, and grinned when she saw her friend, Lucy, running toward her, two girls in tow.

"Oh my goodness," Jill cried, scooping the youngest up in her arms. "Abbe, you're getting so big!" she cooed to the little girl. Abbe hid a shy smile in Jill's shoulder, then peeked out to see if Jill was still watching. "So what are you up to today?" she asked her friend.

"I'm taking Cassie to find a Halloween costume. The kindergarten parade is this Friday," Lucy said. "Hold on, Cassie, we'll go in a moment," she said as her daughter pulled on her hand.

"Kindergarten? Time passes too fast," Jill said. A wistful smile crossed her lips, and she closed her eyes to breathe it away. When she opened them, she smiled at Lucy, hoping she didn't notice. Lucy reached out and squeezed her hand.

"How are you doing?" she asked. Jill kept her smile in place, waving her hand as if it would chase the sadness away.

"I'm doing well, we both are," she said honestly. "There are still some rough days, and I suspect there always will be. But this project we've started has saved me."

"I'm glad to hear. And I'm so proud of you!" she exclaimed. "I'm sorry I missed helping out this time. Please let me know what I can do before the next event happens."

"Every third Friday!" Jill said. "But I could also use some help with flyers and baking beforehand."

"I'm your girl. But I'm afraid today I'm not," she laughed, nearly falling over as Cassie pulled harder. "Okay, sweetie, you've made your point." She took Abbe from Jill's arms and waved goodbye. "Let's catch up soon, okay!" she called as they left.

Jill turned back to the tent, noticing that things were winding down. Oliver sat in The Toby Project, singing silly songs to a group of kids laughing at his feet. The hair stylists were cleaning up their stations and beginning to tear down. Michael was handing out the last few sandwiches and waters. Jill rushed over to him and grabbed two.

"I'll be right back, okay?" she said. He smiled and nodded, turning his attention back to the small line at his table.

Jill headed to the back of the restaurant, looking around until she saw two feet poking out under a tree on a little hill. She'd never spoken to the man, but knew he was there. She walked forward, holding the sandwich out.

"Here you go, sir," she said gently. He peeked out from where the branches hid him, his eyes wide. But when he saw the sandwich, his face broke into a toothless grin, his eyes narrowing with happiness. He took the sandwich, nodding his thank you. Then he hid back under the tree so that all she could see were his wiggling feet as he ate.

Jill returned to the parking lot and made her way over to where Albert was sitting. Rusty's blanket lay at his feet, only the bunny ears on top of it. Albert was still slumped in his chair. But when Jill came over, he didn't move at all.

"Albert?" she whispered. He opened his eyes, terror filling them as he looked at her. He opened his mouth to speak, but no words came. His head rolled forward, and she reached out to catch him. "Albert, you okay?" she asked. He said nothing, but he breathed out in hard spurts, as if he were pushing every breath out of him. She looked around as people walked by. They stared at her, but kept walking. "Someone get help!" she called out. She reached in her pocket for her phone, cursing when she realized she'd left it in her purse at the booth. A man walked by and she grabbed his arm. He looked down at her hand on his, then gave her an annoyed look. Jill stood her ground. "There is a man here who is really sick. Please go inside the store and ask the manager to call for help." The man looked at Albert, then back to Jill. His face softened and he nodded before going in. Ten long minutes later, and sirens could be heard from down the street. The emergency vehicle pulled up in front of them.

"His name is Albert," Jill told the EMT. They placed him on the gurney and strapped him on. Albert's eyes widened and he fought with weakened movements. Jill held her hand over her mouth, feeling like she wanted to cry as the EMTs tried to restrain him. She wanted to help him, but she didn't know what to do.

The empty wheelchair remained next to her, the blanket still on the ground. It suddenly occurred to her why the old man was panicking. Jill sprang forward and grabbed the bunny ears off the blanket. Then she placed them in Albert's flailing hands. He stilled, grasping the ears. Then he crossed his arms over his chest, holding the costume piece against him as he was loaded into the truck. The door closed behind him, and they were off.

"What just happened?" Michael asked behind her. She turned and threw herself into his arms.

"It's Albert," she said. "They just took him to the hospital." She buried her head in his chest, the reality of what had just happened crushing down on her. "I don't know why this is affecting me like this," she apologized through her tears. "He's never been nice to me. But he's not okay, and I'm really worried about him."

"Come on, let's go," he said, taking her arm.

"But the booth! We have to still tear it down! I can't just abandon everyone!" she cried.

"We got it, girl," Sue said. She and a few others had come over to see what the commotion was all about. "You just find out if he's okay, all right?" Jill nodded, reaching over to squeeze Sue's hand. She ran with Michael over to the booth to grab her purse, offering a quick explanation to Oliver before she left.

"You want to come with?" she asked him. Oliver just shook his head no.

"You know I don't like the guy," he said. "Besides, I can't stand being in a car." He paused and looked up at her. "But if anything happens…" He trailed off.

"I'll let you know," she said. He tilted his head and then focused on fiddling with his guitar.

Jill

~ Twenty-four ~
Rough Around the Edges

The waiting room at the hospital was nearly empty when Jill burst through the sliding doors, Michael close behind. She went straight to the window where a nurse was rifling through papers. Jill tapped on the window, causing the woman to jump. She gave Jill an annoyed glance before sliding the partition over.

"Can I help you?" the woman asked, though her tone suggested she wanted to do anything *but* help her.

"A man came in here just a little while ago," Jill said. "His name is Albert."

"Last name?" the nurse asked. Jill shook her head.

"I don't know," she admitted. The nurse looked through her papers again, but didn't seem to find what she was looking for. Frowning, she got up and left Jill to wait where she was. Jill looked behind her. Michael was already sitting in the chairs that lined the walls. A few feet away, a mother held her child wrapped in a blanket, another child sitting at her feet. In the corner, a man held a towel over his hand, the once-white fabric now pink. The room was quiet, almost too quiet. Jill moved from the window and sat in the chair next to her husband.

"She must be finding where he is," Jill whispered.

"Maybe," Michael said. "But I don't know if they'll even let you in. You're not family."

While they waited, another nurse came out and collected the man with the cloth over her hand.

"We'll call you in soon," the nurse apologized to the woman with the child. The woman nodded, rocking her child back and forth. Jill got a look at the boy. He appeared to be about eight or nine, his skin pale except for two very rosy cheeks. He remained asleep in his mother's arms, and she just continued to rock him. Her face remained calm, as if being in the ER was just one of those ordinary things you do when you have a child.

"Are you a friend or family of Mr. Cotter?" the nurse behind the counter called out. Michael ribbed Jill, and she looked up to see where he was pointing. She hopped up and went to the window.

"Excuse me?"

"Albert Cotter," the nurse repeated. "Are you related to him?"

"No. I'm not even sure he has any family. He's one of the homeless men living in the shopping center across town." She paused. "How did you know his last name?"

"He had a card in his pocket, stating his name and who to call in case of emergency. I'm afraid we can't let you in. But we've called his daughter and she's on her way. You're welcome to stay here and wait for her, if you'd like."

His daughter. He has a daughter. Jill let that sink in. Albert has a family, and they let him stay on the streets. Jill tried to keep the judgment from creeping in, but she couldn't help it. How could anyone let their father remain homeless?

Jill went back to the chair, shooting her husband a look before he could open his mouth.

"If you say 'I told you so,' I'm kicking you," she said. He laughed.

"I know better," he said, poking her in the ribs. She wriggled away with a grin. Since it was going to take a while, she grabbed the nearest magazine and opened it up, but only flipped the pages without actually seeing what was on them. She set the magazine down and stared at the fish tank that sat near the front of the room. Beside her, Michael played on his phone. Jill leaned against him, keeping her eyes on the circling fish. Her lids grew heavy. Finally, she succumbed, slipping into a light nap.

The hospital doors flew open, and Jill opened her eyes with a start. A tall blonde woman raced in, heading straight for the counter.

"Hi," she said, out of breath. "I'm Julie Cotter, Albert's daughter. Is he here? Is he okay? Can I see him?"

"He's being evaluated right now, so you can't see him yet. Please fill out this paperwork while you wait." The nurse handed her a clipboard. The woman took it, looking at it for a moment with a wrinkled brow. She looked up, noticing she wasn't alone in the waiting room, and composed herself. She went to a chair on the other side of the room.

A man, appearing to be in his early twenties, entered the emergency waiting room, furrowing his scarred brow as he looked around. He saw the woman across the way, and went to sit with her.

"Have they said anything yet?" he asked. He put his hand on her knee in comfort, his dark skin contrasting with the pale color of her legs. He ran his other hand through his jet black hair. The girl shook her head no, then noticed Jill studying them. Jill turned her head away quick, pretending to focus on the fish.

"The doctor's with him right now. They need me to fill out this paperwork before I can even go near him," Jill heard her say. The papers shuffled. "I don't even know half this crap. I haven't seen him in years." Her voice wavered, and Jill could hear her fighting back tears. She turned back around and stood.

"I'll be right back," she said to Michael. He glanced over to where her attention was turned, and then nodded.

"I'll be here if you need me," he told her. Jill squeezed his hand, and then made her way over to the young couple.

"Hi," she said. They both looked up at her, and she felt her cheeks flush. The woman gave her an icy stare, her whole demeanor suggesting the interruption was not welcome. "Sorry," Jill continued, brushing off the woman's look of irritation. "I couldn't help but overhear. My name is Jill, and that's my husband, Michael, over there. I'm the one who called the ambulance about your father." She held out her hand, and felt relieved when the blonde woman relaxed from her guarded state to offer her a warm smile and a handshake.

"Thank you so much," she breathed. "My name's Julie, and this my boyfriend, Ben. Do you know what's wrong with my father?" she asked. Jill shook her head.

"Not exactly. He was sitting slumped in his chair when I found him. As long as I've known him, he's barely eaten anything. He's been drinking a lot, too. But more than that, he just hasn't been doing well since his dog passed away."

"Oh no!" Julie sighed, setting the clipboard in her lap and shaking her head. "Was it a golden retriever?" she asked. Jill nodded. "Poor Rusty," she lamented, her brow furrowed. "Dad loved that old boy."

"Yeah, I think that dog was the only living thing in this world that he did like," Jill said, making Julie smile.

"My dad can be a bit difficult, I guess," Julie said. Her brow furrowed again, and she looked away. Ben patted her knee as she wiped a rogue tear away. "Sorry, it's just been so long since I've seen him. I wasn't even sure if he was alive anymore."

"When was the last time you saw him?" Jill asked.

"It's been years, I'm afraid. He'd always been a drinker, but it got worse when my mom died." She paused, looking up at Jill with a helpless look in her eyes. "He didn't always used to be this way, you know," she explained, a glimmer of guilt washing over her face. "He was smart, worked hard, and provided for all of us. But the bottle always got in his way. It got so bad that I finally took off when I was fourteen. I just couldn't take it anymore. I moved in with my aunt in San Francisco for a time until I was old enough to take care of myself. And my dad, he just went off the deep end. He lost his job, the house, everything. The last time I saw him, I made him wear a laminated card with my contact information on it. You know, just in case…" She trailed off, looking up at the ceiling as her eyes filled with tears.

"Hey," Jill said, taking Julie's hand. "I'm sure he's going to be fine. Albert's a stubborn old mule, he's probably survived worse than this in his life, right?"

"I guess," Julie said, unconvinced. "I don't even know what's wrong with him."

"Why don't we work together on that paperwork you have there," Jill said. She looked over Julie's shoulder and told her what she knew about Albert, which still wasn't much. But at least they were able to fill out more together than Julie was able to do on her own. Julie then marched it over to the nurse at the window.

"Can we see my dad now, please?" she demanded. The nurse looked up and eyed Jill and Ben, and then Michael who walked up behind them.

"I'm sorry, but only family is allowed," the nurse told her.

"We are family," Julie said without batting an eye. "This is my sister, and these are my brothers." Jill could hear Ben hide a snort. The nurse raised her eyebrows, challenging Julie's lie. She then gave just the hint of a smile.

"All right then, fine. You're all family. Still, we can't have you all clogging up the ER. Only two of you will be allowed in at a time.

Jill felt her heart drop. Julie would, of course, be going in, and she would probably want Ben with her. She started to turn back to the chairs when Julie grabbed her arm.

"Would you guys mind waiting out here while Jill and I go see my, er, our dad?" Julie asked.

"Go on," Michael said. "I don't mind waiting." He winked at his wife. Jill wanted to kiss him for being so kind, for coming here with her and sticking around, for supporting her in this and everything that was important to her. But kissing him would probably be weird since they just said they were brother and sister. So she winked back, grinning at him.

"I don't mind waiting, either," Ben said. He wasn't so discreet, and gave Julie's hand a tender squeeze and a kiss on the cheek, awfully close to her mouth.

"I'll get you when I come out," Jill promised, and she followed Julie and the nurse through the door into the emergency area.

Albert's eyes were closed when the two women walked in. He was surrounded by tubes and machines, a heart monitor next to him beeping in time with his heartbeat. An IV with clear liquid hung from a pole, a tube connecting to his arm. Jill felt a tickle in her throat and cleared it as quietly as she could. Still, the sudden sound made Albert's eyes drift open. He turned in the direction of the noise, his eyes resting on Jill. He snorted when he realized who she was.

"What're you doing here," he grunted. Jill smiled, noting that grouchiness must be a good sign.

"Same old Albert," she laughed. He grunted again. Then his eyes softened, looking just beyond her at the woman who hung back against the wall.

"Julie," he whispered.

"Hi, Dad," she said softly, the tall willowy blonde suddenly taking on a shy demeanor. Jill watched as Julie became like a little girl, her smile bordering on hurt and fear….and hope. She came next to her dad's bedside, taking his hand in hers. The contrast between his weathered skin and her soft pale hands was hard to miss. He was rough around the edges, Julie was neat and tidy. There next to each other, it was like he was night, and she was day. But if Julie noticed anything wrong with her father's appearance, she showed no sign. She crossed the invisible barrier between those with and those without, giving her dad a soft kiss on the forehead with the tenderness of a child.

"Dad, next time you want me to come find you, can you just pick up the phone and call?" He gave her a weak smile—the first smile Jill had ever seen him give the entire time she'd known him.

"It's so good to see you, Julie," he said, his old eyes glistening, even as the smile remained on his crooked mouth.

Maddie

- Twenty-five -
No Other Choice

The baby fell asleep while nursing, and Maddie slowly lowered her from her chest and covered herself back up. She laid Hope gently on the ground so as to not wake her, then moved to stand. Her legs felt shaky as she placed one foot down, using her knee to hoist herself up. She felt the blood drain from her head, and she paused to wait out the dizziness that followed. Her body ached, and all she wanted to do was curl up in the weeds and fall asleep. It would be so easy, just lay down and fall asleep. But she needed to move, or she'd never have the courage to follow through.

Maddie picked up her bag, slinging it over her shoulder. Then she leaned down, carefully scooping Hope into her arms, pulling the blanket tighter around her so she wouldn't be cold. The sky was beginning to darken. She wondered where the young boy had gone. He had told her he was getting help, but that was over an hour ago. She was glad he never came back. She didn't need him, or anyone. She didn't need the Winstons. She didn't need Jordan or her parents, or anyone else that would just let her down.

She knew her place, she knew where she belonged. And she knew where Hope belonged.

She made her way through the tall weeds, stepping carefully so as to not wake the baby. She reached the end of the row of vines and turned right. The road was a straight shot ahead. Maddie continued to walk with careful steps, looking behind her every few minutes to make sure no one was following her.

The road loomed in front of her, and Maddie stepped onto the hard pavement. The cars rushed past her, their headlights blinding her every time they passed. Night had fallen, and the fog hung in the air around her like a heavy blanket. Maddie shivered from the cold, pulling Hope closer to her body to keep the both of them warm.

The fire station stood out in the fog like a beacon, its red and white lights glowing bright within the fog. Maddie's heart raced as she walked forward. As she walked, she prayed. It seemed that once she opened that fountain, it was going to pour and pour. *Please God. Please give me strength. Please don't leave me in this.*

Her arm felt heavy as she lifted it, bringing her clenched fist against the solid door of the fire station. The sound echoed into the night, through her head, against her closed hand. She prayed no one would be there, that she could turn around and have enough time to come up with a new plan. Her heart fell when she saw a shadow against the tempered glass window of the door. The door opened, and a man in a blue fireman's uniform gave her a kind smile. Inside, it appeared that every light was on. The station looked so warm, so inviting. This was the right choice. This was the only choice.

"Good evening, Miss," he said. "How can I help you?" She opened her mouth to speak, but no words came out. She tried, but it was like she had forgotten how to talk. Shaking, she shifted Hope in her arms, then lifted her up to the fireman. She could feel the catch in her throat and the tears threatening her eyes. But she fought against them as she held the baby girl out to the man in front of her. He looked down at the child, his arms moving forward to take the bundle she was offering him. His face was filled with bewilderment, now holding the tiny infant in his arms. Maddie pulled her arms away, pulling them into her chest to suppress the sob forming in her throat and the emptiness she felt in her whole being.

"Are you sure about this?" he asked. The compassion in his face made Maddie turn away. Was she sure about this? *No.* She looked back at the fireman who now held her daughter. There were a million things she wanted to say. She wasn't sure. She wanted to keep Hope in her care forever. She wanted a house to live in and a crib to lay her daughter in every night. She wanted to be there when Hope laughed for the first time, said her first word, and took her first steps. She wanted to hold her daughter and tell her everything was okay the first time she suffered a broken heart, and to cheer her on from the sidelines when she scored her first soccer goal. She wanted to be the kind of parent her mother and father weren't, standing behind her little girl through thick and thin, loving her through it all.

But she also wanted her daughter to be well-cared for, to have all the things she didn't have. She wanted her to be safe. She wanted her to grow up never knowing what it was like to suffer. If she kept Hope, her daughter would never have any of that.

She glanced at the baby, so tiny and perfect in the fireman's arms. Her face was hidden, but Maddie could see the mass of black hair that peeked out from behind the blanket. She longed to reach out and touch it, just to see if she could memorize its downy texture. But she kept her hands folded in at her chest, stepping back. She looked up at the officer, and nodded. His eyes fell, but he nodded back to her.

It was done.

She turned and ran, her body screaming as the adrenaline hit her and carried her to the road. She could hear the firefighter calling out to her, but she didn't look back. As she ran, her bag swung against her legs, the weight from the jar of money hitting her in the legs. Her heart dropped. She had meant to leave that with Hope, to give her something to take with her when she was placed with new parents. She stopped, turning around to go back. Then she stopped again. If she went back, she'd never be able to leave again. But the money wasn't hers. She had been saving it all this time so she had something to take care of her daughter with. Now that her daughter was gone, she didn't want it.

Maddie looked up at the swirling fog around her. She felt completely alone, as if the world around her had disappeared. If it weren't for the white stripe that bordered the right side of the road, she wouldn't know which way to walk. Still, she felt lost. She dropped the bag on the ground and opened her mouth. It scared her how loud her scream was as she yelled into the silent mist around her. Her heart leapt into her throat as she cried out, cursing the pain that was wrenching inside her. She dropped to her knees on the side of the road, banging against the rough asphalt with her fists. The pain coursed through her—pain she had control over. It relieved a small portion of the anguish that tore her up inside.

The jar still lay inside the bag, and Maddie pulled it out. Gripping the glass, she hurled it across the street. The jar shattered all along the asphalt, becoming diamonds against the dark ground, the bills fluttering in a wind she couldn't feel. She watched the money she had saved for months drift in all different directions. It felt both freeing and terrifying to watch all her hard work scatter as if it never existed.

Now she had nothing.

She picked herself up off the ground, leaving the empty bag to decay on the side of the road, and ran as fast as she could. Her feet pounded the pavement with each step, stumbling in forceful blows. She shouldn't be running. She knew this. Her body was throbbing from the trauma of giving birth. Her lungs screamed at her, begging her to stop. The cold fog pelted her skin, slapping at her with each gust of wind. But the ache in her heart felt worst.

The yellow sign appeared through the mist, indicating a right turn would lead her to the vineyards. She reached it and began to walk the gravel road that led to the house.

But then she stopped. Where was she going? How would she face them? What was she even going to tell them?

Maddie dropped to her knees, the reality of what she had just done overwhelming her. She shook, the tears she'd been holding back now unstoppable. She cried into her hands, collapsing against her bent legs, folded up on the dirt road as her heart broke open inside her.

She never noticed the headlights of the car that came toward her, but she heard the gravel crunch under its tires as it slowed to a stop next to her. She didn't move, sobbing uncontrollably as the door to the car opened and closed, and a pair of boots walked over to her. She felt warm arms wrap around her, rocking her back and forth as she cried.

"Shhh," Mr. Winston whispered into her hair. "It's going to be okay. It's going to be okay." He said it over and over again, just as the boy had done when she was at her most helpless. He rocked her with each stanza of the hypnotic prayer, and she melted into his arms, letting him be her strength as she cried into his chest.

"I couldn't keep her," she finally mustered, wiping her nose against his scratchy flannel.

"Shhh…" he repeated. He kissed the top of her head and then stood. With surprising strength, the elderly man lifted her as if she weighed nothing, bringing her to the car. He opened the car door with one hand, sat her in the front seat, and then buckled her in like she was a child. Exhausted, Maddie didn't fight him or try to do it on her own. She needed someone else to be in charge for a while. She needed to be taken care of. Mr. Winston patted her knee once he was in the driver's seat. Then he put the car in drive, turning it around and heading back up the road to the house.

"You'll sleep here tonight," he said when they were safe inside the lit up house. He hung his hat on the hook next to the door, then removed his jacket.

"But my mother…" Maddie started, attempting to keep up the charade. Mr. Winston gave her a tired smile.

"If there's someone you need to call, you can use the phone in my study," he said. By the look on his face, Maddie could tell he was aware there was no one for her to call. She looked at the floor, ashamed that he knew her secret. "I'll bring you to your room," he said.

Maddie followed him up the stairs. The guest room was already made up, the light blue sheets of the bed turned down as if they had expected her to stay. A pair of Mrs. Winston's pajamas lay folded on the edge of the bed, the material a soft flowered flannel. Maddie was relieved to see some pads partially concealed underneath the clothes. Mr. Winston bid her goodnight and closed the door behind him, giving her time alone. Maddie took a moment to look around. It was only for the night, but it still felt unreal. A room of her own. Tonight there would be no dumpster, no restaurant, no parking lot or hard asphalt. There would be no worries about food, or how to stay warm, or where to hide if it rained. There was just a room with a window, a door to the bathroom, and a plush bed with more blankets than she'd slept under in months.

And no Hope.

Maddie closed her eyes and breathed. It was for the best. *It's for her.* She repeated this over and over. *For her. For her.* It was the only thing keeping her from breaking open.

She turned on the water in the attached bathroom, stripping out of her soiled clothing and slipping into the hot water. The clear water turned a murky red from the grime, sweat, and blood on her body. But she didn't care. The water felt good, relaxing. She drifted down into the water, letting it engulf her body until even her face was underwater. The silence was delicious, just the sound of her own heartbeat in her ears. She stayed there for a moment, letting her lungs burn in protest. *What if I stay this way? What if I never come up for air?* It was a tempting thought—one that only lasted as long as her lungs would let her. She came back up out of the water, gulping in one huge breath to make up for the ones she lost. Then she leaned against the back of the tub, getting drunk off the warmth in the water. Her belly was still swollen, almost as if there was still a baby in there. She lay her hands on it, missing the hardness it once possessed, and the little kicks of greeting her daughter used to give her. It felt strange for it to be so still, so empty...so lifeless.

With sleepy movements, Maddie lathered soap all over her body, wiping away the dirt and regret that had covered her for months. She kept it up until the water cooled. Then she let the water drain and dried herself off with the fluffy blue towel hanging on the back of the door. She put the pajamas on and brushed her teeth, realizing what an exquisite feeling it was to have clean teeth again. She slid in between the cool sheets, sure that she had never felt anything so good—not even the bath. The bed was a vast difference from the way she had been sleeping for months. She felt like she might fall into the mattress, feeling hugged on all sides by the plush cushion underneath her.

The distant spotlight from the vineyards bathed her room in a comforting glow, chasing out the dark and the fear of being alone. She watched it from her pillow, feeling her eyes grow heavy. It only took a few moments for her to slip out of consciousness, falling into a deep sleep until morning.

Maddie

~ Twenty-six ~
The Scent of Home

Maddie could smell bacon frying when she woke up. For a second she thought she was back home in her old room. She smiled at the thought, until she remembered why she didn't live there anymore. Her hands flew to her stomach, her eyes filling with tears when all the previous day's events came flooding in.

Her baby was gone. *Oh God. I made a mistake.*

She sat up quick. A wave of dizziness washed over her, pain racking every muscle in her body. She felt like she'd been hit by a truck. She got out of bed, crossing the room to look in the mirror. The girl who looked back at her was a stranger. Her face was thinner, her cheeks gaunt. Her brown eyes were hidden within dark circles, almost as if they were bruised. Her full lips were cracked from being so chapped. Her long, dark hair seemed to envelop her small frame, both matted and curly from sleeping on it wet.

She pulled her hair back into a knot and grabbed a robe out of the closet in the room. Opening the door, she padded down the stairs. Mr. Winston smiled up at her from over his newspaper at the kitchen table. Mrs. Winston was cooking breakfast at the stove, humming while the morning sunlight streamed in across the vineyards and through the kitchen window.

"Maddie, darling!" Mrs. Winston said as Maddie came within view. "I'm so glad you're up. Would you like two or three pieces of bacon with your pancakes? Or maybe more?" The elderly woman held her spatula like a pointer, waiting for Maddie's answer.

"Two is good," she said, her stomach rumbling. She hadn't eaten anything since breakfast the day before, and her body was suddenly remembering. She sat down at the table, looking at the stained wood of the surface, not sure where else to look. She felt like an intruder, embarrassed to even be there. It was Saturday. She should be back at the parking lot, and the Winstons should have time to themselves. At the very least, she should be serving them, not the other way around.

Mrs. Winston set a steaming stack of pancakes in front of her, several pieces of bacon to the side, and a pitcher of warmed syrup for the center of the table. She then added two more plates, one in her spot and one for Mr. Winston. Maddie picked at her food, cutting a small triangle of pancakes and spearing it with her fork. Then she brought the fork to her mouth, letting herself savor the soft bread of the pancakes and the sweet stickiness of the syrup. It was delicious. She fought the urge to shovel the food in her mouth, ignoring her growling stomach as she took small bite after small bite. Her plate was empty too soon. Before she could clear it, Mr. Winston stacked three more pancakes on it, adding a few more slices of bacon.

"But I couldn't possibly…"

"Eat," he ordered her, a smile in his eyes. Maddie looked down, grinning into her plate. Then she started in on her second plate.

"We need to talk about yesterday," he told her. The smile was gone from his eyes, and his face took on a look of seriousness.

"Yessir," she said, looking at her plate again. This time she set her fork on the plate and folded her hands in her lap.

"When you rushed out yesterday, I thought you had been disgusted by everything I told you about Ellie," he said quietly. Maddie looked up, alarmed.

"No, Mr. Winston, that's not what happened!" she insisted. "I felt terrible for you! You loved her so much, and she was so awful to you. And then to have lost her that way… Mr. Winston, I never thought it was your fault."

"I know that now," Mr. Winston said. "At least, it's not really important what your thoughts were about it. What matters is what happened afterwards."

"Mr. Winston, I'm so sorry. I didn't know it was happening. I just felt so sick, and I was embarrassed. I wanted to hide. And then I was so far away from everyone when I realized what was happening. If it hadn't been for the boy…"

"Boy? What boy?"

"The boy! He must have been one of the workers' sons or something. He didn't speak English. But he stayed with me the whole time, helping me give birth to Hope."

"Hope?"

Maddie looked down at the table, tears filling her eyes. "The baby. That's what I named her before.... Oh God, I did something terrible. Or wonderful. I don't know. I just wanted her to be safe, to not have to be a part of what my life looks like. I wanted her to have a clean slate, to start over fresh, to have..."

"Hope," Mrs. Winston finished, her voice lighting into the conversation like the song of a bird. Maddie looked at the woman, tears in her eyes.

"Mrs. Winston, have you ever loved someone so much, you felt like your heart was going to just beat right out of your chest?" Maddie whispered.

"Every day, darling," Mrs. Winston said. From her sweater pocket, she pulled out a small picture frame and handed it over. Maddie took it and looked. In it were three people—a much younger Mr. and Mrs. Winston, and a small girl in Mrs. Winston's arms, her blonde hair in ringlets and her finger pointing at the person taking the picture. Maddie studied it for a moment, searching the faces for any signs of the anguish to come. There was none.

"Mr. Winston, if the boy didn't find you, how did you know where to find me?" Maddie asked.

"One of the firemen called the house. They put two and two together and figured you were one of our employees."

"But the boy!" Maddie insisted. "He said he was going to get help. He didn't find you?"

"Maddie, I don't know who you're talking about. None of the workers were here. Harvest ended. I didn't hire anyone to come work the fields yesterday."

"But I don't understand…" Maddie said. He was there. She knew it. "He kept telling me it would be okay. He said it over and over again. He stayed with me, and then he said he was going to get help." Maddie then remembered the sweatshirt in the vines. "He left his sweatshirt!" she exclaimed. She got up from the table and flew out the door, barreling down steps. Her body complained, reminding her she hadn't yet recovered, so she slowed to a jog. She searched up one row of vines, then down the next. She could see Mr. Winston standing at the bottom, watching her as she zigzagged in search of the blue sweatshirt. But when she had gone further than she knew she'd been, she stopped. She walked back down the hill, her head down.

"I swear, Mr. Winston, it was there. He was there," she said.

"I believe you," he said. But she knew that he didn't.

"Maybe it was your guardian angel," Mrs. Winston piped up from behind her husband, siding up to him and linking her arm through his. Maddie smiled at the thought. It wasn't true. It couldn't be. Maybe?

"It was probably just a neighbor who happened to be nearby," Maddie said, even though they all knew their closest neighbors were the firemen in the station down the road.

Once in the house, Mr. Winston sat them all back down at the table in the kitchen. He folded his hands in front of him and looked at Maddie.

"We have some things to discuss," he said. She nodded. Was this the part where he told her what a horrible person she was for giving away her baby, tossing her aside like a piece of trash—like her parents had? She lowered her gaze to her lap, her eyes filling with tears.

"I was scared, Mr. Winston," she said. "I didn't know what to do. My life is so messed up right now, and I couldn't bring her into this. My parents want nothing to do with me, her father took off on us, and I have nothing to offer her. I couldn't do that to her. I love her too much to give her a life like this. She deserves better."

"What you did was brave, Maddie," Mr. Winston said, reaching forward to take her hand.

"Brave?" Maddie cried, snatching her hand back. "I was a coward! I was afraid! I handed her off to some stranger because I couldn't handle taking care of her myself!"

"No, you acted out of love. You were brave, and you were selfless. You acted like that little girl's mother."

"I don't feel like a mother," Maddie said, tears falling into her lap.

"Would you like to be?" he asked. Mrs. Winston reached over and took Maddie's hand, stroking it with her thumb. She looked over at her husband and smiled, and he looked at her and winked. Then they both turned their attention to Maddie.

"I have some options for you. The first one is not exactly an option, but a demand. You are to live here with us. The room you slept in will be yours. I'll take you shopping for some clothes when you feel up to it. And we'll sign you up for classes at the high school nearby."

"But Mr. Winston," she began.

"No buts. We've been talking about this for weeks now, and have just been waiting for the right time to approach you about this. I can't think of any better time than now. Move in with us, it would make us so happy."

Maddie looked at both of them. They smiled, waiting for her to agree. *A home. A real life home, with a family who wants me here.* Slowly, Maddie mirrored their smiles with one on her lips, nodding. The couple exclaimed, pulling Maddie close as they hugged across the table.

"Now for your other option," Mr. Winston said. "And this isn't as easy of a decision." He held something in his hand, looking down at it and then handing it to her. It was a blue bracelet, the name 'Alice' on it. "Joe, the firefighter who took Hope in, didn't know the baby's name," Mr. Winston said. "It's the name of his mother."

"What is this?" Maddie asked.

"It's a bracelet. Hope is wearing a matching one around her ankle. It links the two of you. With it, you have two weeks to decide whether this is the decision you want to make. Without it, there's no easy proof that you're her mother, and she becomes a ward of the state."

Maddie looked at the bracelet, not sure what to do. When she thought her decision was final, she was sure she'd made the biggest mistake of her life. But now, holding the life line that kept her tied to Hope, she didn't know what to think. She had a home now, and the Winstons were wonderful people. By the looks on their faces, she knew they would welcome another mouth to feed with open arms. But was that the best for Hope? And was she ready to be a mother? She was only sixteen, still a child herself. Was it smart to take Hope back? Was it better for her to be with her birth mother rather than two parents who could provide for her without the help of strangers?

Maddie didn't know.

"Like I said, you have time to think about it," Mr. Winston said. "It's a huge decision, and we will support you, no matter what you decide."

Maddie nodded, slipping the bracelet into her pocket. She stood, gathering the plates that still lay across the table. When Mrs. Winston tried to wave her away, Maddie stopped her.

"Please, let me do it," she said. Mrs. Winston smiled and sat back down.

Maddie brought all the plates to the counter and filled the sink with soapy water. She looked out the window, watching as the October sun cast its rays on the golden leaves of the vines. The tree just outside the window only had a few leaves left, a few more falling when a bird lit upon the branch. It cocked its head, seeming to look at Maddie on the other side of the window. Then it flew away. The brilliant blue of the sky met the deep yellow and orange hues of the vineyard, the entire scene painted into Maddie's memory, forever, she was sure.

Maddie breathed in deep, inhaling the scent of breakfast and dish soap, clean laundry and wood floors, sunshine and a room filled with love. It smelled like home.

She was home.

Jill

~ Twenty-seven ~
Ready or Not

"So, it seems Albert was just suffering from severe dehydration from too much alcohol and not enough food," Jill said. She took a sip of her coffee, still reeling from the night before. She and Michael hadn't made it home until late, crawling into bed as soon as they walked in the door. They hadn't even had the energy to rehash the whole day. But with the sunshine casting its light through the window of their bedroom, they paused in bed with their coffee cups, reliving the events of the day before.

"What a day yesterday was," she sighed.

"You got that right," Michael agreed. "So what happens to him now?"

"It's hard to say," Jill said. "Julie mentioned bringing him home."

"Wow. Do you think that's smart? I mean, that can't be an easy transition for either of them, I'm sure."

"I know. From what it sounds like, they don't have the closest relationship. There's a lot of baggage there. But Julie did mention how it might help keep her boyfriend from inviting more people to live at her house. Did you know the last ones stole all her rent money?"

"That's rough!" Michael said, shaking his head. "But now she's inviting some homeless guy to live with her? How does she know he won't do the same?"

"I doubt Albert would do that," Jill said.

"Jill, you're always so trusting. I think that's what I love most about you, how you always want to see the good in everyone."

"I do not! I hate people, too!" she laughed.

"Right. Like Albert, who threw your sandwich to his dog, or the girl who changed your life by breaking your arm," he teased her. Jill wrinkled her nose with a smile.

"Okay, fine. I guess I'm a big softie."

"Well, don't change. I kind of like you that way."

"What way?"

He leaned over and kissed her forehead, then looked into her face. Her eyes connected with his, and she felt a pulse of electricity as she held his gaze. She could never get tired of this, of the way he loved her, and the way she loved him back. He leaned down and pressed his lips to hers, grazing them with the most gentle touch.

"The way you're so soft," he whispered against her mouth. She laughed, but then stopped when she remembered the gift box in her purse. Her heart skipped a beat at the thought of it.

"Don't move a muscle!" she exclaimed, jumping up to throw on a robe, then running into the other room to grab her purse. She came back, rummaging through it until her hand met the smooth edges of the wrapped gift. She handed it to him with a grin. "I can't believe I almost forgot to give you this," she said. "I meant to give it to you yesterday, when Maddie's Mission was over. But with Albert and everything…"

"What is it?" he asked, shaking it and holding it to his ear. Jill laughed.

"Well, it's not going to talk. You probably should open it."

Michael fiddled with the ribbon, using his teeth to get the knot undone. Then he worked on the paper, tearing it away until just the box remained. He opened it, and his eyes went wide. Then he looked at her. Jill held her breath, the silence in the room interrupted only by the ticking of the clock on her dresser.

"Are you sure?" he asked her, and she nodded. He picked up the pregnancy test, the large plus sign on it louder than a billboard.

"That's the fourth test I took," she said. "I think it's safe to say we're pregnant!"

Jill watched for his reaction. She, herself, had many mixed feelings about this. Would the new baby make her forget Toby? She was scared that would happen, that a new child would somehow become a replacement for Toby as if he had never existed. And she was afraid that this child growing inside her would be raised in the shadows of Toby, feeling compared to a ghost he had never met. Could she handle the balance of honoring Toby's memory without taking away from the life of this child?

But more than all that, Jill was elated. She had missed being a mother. She had thought that role had ended when

Toby died. But being a mother was in her bones. Even without a child, she was still a mother. Losing him didn't take that away. The realization that she was being given a second chance at holding her own child in her arms, raising him or her with all the love she had to offer…it completed the sentence of her life.

Michael sat still in the bed next to her, staring at the pregnancy test in his hands. He was quiet when Jill leaned into him.

"What are you thinking?" she asked him. He sighed, placing the test on his lap.

"I was thinking about how much I miss Toby," he said. "I miss having him here to make noise while we're eating, or how he used to complain when we didn't pick him up exactly when he wanted us to. I miss how his face would get messy, no matter what he was eating, how he would put so much energy into his meal that it would end up exploding all over his chubby cheeks."

Jill laughed quietly as he spoke, a mark of sadness sitting heavy on her heart. Michael's eyes were watery, and he sighed, then offered his wife a small smile.

"I miss swinging him around in the yard," he continued. "I miss the way he'd squeal each time I did it, as if it was the first time. And I miss holding him close when he fell asleep, the way his body would just relax into mine. I miss that we never got to see him grow up, that we never got to see what kind of man our little boy was going to be."

Michael paused, taking Jill's hand in his, the tears now rolling down his cheeks.

"But I'm also thinking about how much I miss being a dad—not just Toby's dad, but a *dad*. I miss that feeling of having this little being trust me so much with their life, holding my hand as if that is enough to keep them safe."

He looked down at the pregnancy test again, seeming to study it. He then squeezed her hands, looking into her face, a smile creeping onto his lips.

"Oh my God," he whispered. "We're having a baby!" Jill laughed through her tears, squeezing his hand in hers.

"Are you scared?" she asked.

"Terrified!" he said with a wince and a small smile. "It seems different going into this now. It's like, I realize now how fragile life is. It's hard not to think about all the things that could go wrong, you know?" Jill nodded in agreement. It was exactly how she felt. "But if you push all that stuff away, it's also hard not to get excited about this. A baby! Wow."

"So you're okay with this?" Jill asked. He turned toward her, taking her face in his hands.

"I'm more than okay with this," he said, looking down into her face. "You are a beautiful woman, you know that Jill? Just beautiful." He leaned toward her and pressed his lips to hers. She tasted his salty tears through his kiss, his tears mingling with her own, just like the sadness in her heart was mingling with the excitement of this new arrival.

A baby. Was she ready? Was he?

Jill rested her head on his chest, looking out the open bedroom door toward Toby's. She could almost hear his laughter coming from his room, and see the joy radiating from his olive eyes as he called to her from his crib. She wondered if he could see them now, if he knew they were preparing to welcome his little brother or sister. Perhaps he would be like a guardian angel to this new baby. The thought gave her comfort.

"Ready or not," she whispered into Michael's chest. "Here you come."

A few weeks later, the careful excitement they felt about having a baby made way for pure elation. Her first doctor's appointment revealed a healthy beating heart, and a due date for the middle of summer. When they left the doctor's, Jill talked Michael into going to the baby store to search for a new crib. She would be losing her art studio, but it didn't feel like a loss. The room was meant for their child. A crib would make it seem more real.

Jill perused the different styles of cribs in the center of the store, smiling at the color schemes that complimented the smooth wooden beds. Would they go with pink, or blue? Or maybe they should go with a more neutral color, like a happy shade of yellow or orange. She let her hand pass over the dark wood of one bed, imagining their baby sleeping on the mattress inside.

"Maybe this one?" she asked Michael. He paused on the other side of it, inspecting the width of the slats, and shaking it to check for sturdiness.

"It's nice," he agreed. "I like how the sides curve like a sleigh bed." He looked up at the mobile that hung over it, a delicate display of small white bunnies floating above the bed. He reached up and touched it, and the bunnies danced around in the air. "I wonder if we'll be having a boy or a girl," he mused.

They looked a little more around the store, but nothing seemed to appeal to them more than the espresso sleigh crib. Soon it was ordered, promised to be shipped to them within the next several weeks. They left for the store exit, Jill holding a bag that carried the bunny mobile within it.

Michael held the door open and Jill went out. She narrowly missed running into someone just outside the store.

"Oh, excuse me!" she apologized, then looked up. She caught herself looking into a familiar face, one she'd seen before. It took her a moment to place where she knew her from. But then it hit her.

Maddie.

The girl's face was a little fuller, her brown eyes brighter than the last time Jill had seen her, and her hair in a neat ponytail. She wore a clean dress, fitting loosely over her small frame, yet tight enough for Jill to see that she was no longer pregnant. She also no longer looked lost or broken. An elderly man came up behind her, resting his hand on the girl's shoulder. Jill watched as Maddie looked up at him, giving him a small smile, then returned to look at Jill, the smile still on her face. Jill looked around them, wondering where Maddie's baby was. Then she looked back at the girl, an unspoken question in her eyes.

"You ready?" Michael asked, taking Jill's hand. "Pardon us," he said to the girl, unaware of who she was. Jill allowed herself to be led away, unable to bring herself to say anything more. It wasn't necessary. The girl was taken care of, as she could see by the man who stayed near her, his presence like that of a father or grandfather.

She turned back around as they passed an elderly woman, pushing a stroller with a tiny bundle wrapped within a familiar blanket of green and purple squares.

"Wait up, you two," the woman called out past Jill and Michael. "We're just a little bit slower." Jill's eyes followed the woman as she made her way to Maddie and the old man, who was holding the door open for them. And she smiled as the three of them, the baby in the stroller, and a blanket filled with memories and lullabies all entered the baby store together.

It seemed that hope had found them all.

The end.

Acknowledgments

On November 1, 2011, I embarked on a writing adventure called NaNoWriMo, also known as National Novel Writing Month. The goal was to reach 50,000 words by November 30th, and I was bound and determined to meet that goal.

During those thirty days, I poured my heart out in a reckless rough draft that mingled real life with fiction, unleashing a few hurts and hardships I'd suffered in life—the death of a child, poverty, young pregnancy, heartbreak—and allowed my characters to suffer on my behalf while I healed. In doing so, I fell in love with Maddie and Jill, two women who suffered terrible loss and found strength in the rebuilding of their lives. This book will always be a personal love story to myself, telling the truth that light can always emerge even in the darkest of times.

My heartfelt thanks goes first and foremost to my husband, Shawn, who read my roughest draft of this story on December 1 (a practice I don't recommend, by the way), and loved it despite all of its grammatical errors and storyline flaws. Thank you for always standing behind me and believing in me. I love you bigger than the sky.

I want to thank my editor, Nancy McLerran, who also gave birth to me a few decades ago. I am so fortunate to have a mother/editor who can smooth out my story both with love and brutal honesty so that I put forth the best novel possible.

I want to thank my early readers and dear friends—Liz Carrasco, Kathe Gerhardt Carpenter, Tahryn Anderson, Alberto Melendez, and Katie Talbot. You each offered me valuable insight that helped add a new dimension to this story.

A most sincere thank you to Liz Carrasco for her saint-like patience and eye for design in the creation of this story's book cover. And thank you to Kent Sorensen for the use of his gorgeous vineyard photo on the front cover. Come to Sonoma County, everyone. These vineyards are everywhere!

Many thanks go to the Redwood Writers. Your support has helped me grow by leaps and bounds!

I want to thank my children—Summer, Lucas, and Andrew. The teen years are not the easiest to have patience, and yet you allowed me the space to check out while I worked on this book. I love you all.

A huge thank you to my supportive family—Gary McLerran, Elsie Chretien, Melissa Moreno, Heather McLerran, Brian Moreno, Joan O'Connor, Dave O'Connor, Anne Schmidbauer, Pam Enquist, and the rest of my huge extended family. Thank you for being my biggest and loudest cheering squad!

And thank you to each of my readers! Discovering how my stories have touched you feeds my desire to keep writing. I read each and every review, comment, email, and letter sent to me from readers about my books, and I couldn't be more grateful for your words. Thank you, from the bottom of my heart. Don't ever quench your passion for literacy. Keep reading!

Crissi Langwell's Books

Hope at the Crossroads (Book 2 of the Hope series)

No longer homeless, Maddie is ready for a promising future. Her new family loves and supports her as a single mother, college is on the horizon, and with a brand new relationship, this summer is sure to be the start of something wonderful. But when a face from her past comes back into her life, Maddie has some decisions to make—and her choice will change everything.

Hope for the Broken Girl (Book 3 of the Hope series)

He promised to take care of her. He promised to be a good father to Hope. He promised she'd have everything she ever wanted. He lied. (Coming in 2017)

Loving the Wind: The Story of Tiger Lily & Peter Pan

Neverland is seen through the eyes of Tiger Lily, the princess of the Miakoda Tribe. Her people share legends of the boy who flies like the birds, lives with the fairies, and harbors a stolen moon. But Tiger Lily never believed the stories were true until she comes face-to-face with Peter Pan aboard Captain Hook's ship. Worse, the flying thief seems to have stolen her heart.

Come Here, Cupcake (Book 1 of the Dessert for Dinner series)

Morgan Truly never wanted to come home to Bodega Bay. But when her mother takes a turn for the worse, Morgan packs up her life in Seattle and heads back to her sleepy coastal hometown, taking on a job at the local dessert shop. However, she soon learns there are a few perks to being home. First, there's that rugged sailor who can't seem to get enough of her sweets. And second, no one else can either—because who can resist enchanted desserts? Morgan discovers she has magical abilities that involve her baking. Unfortunately, her magic is the very thing that could take her happiness away.

A Symphony of Cicadas (Book 1 of the Forever After series)

Cast into the afterlife, Rachel Ashby is left helpless to witness the remnants of the life she left behind and the undoing of her fiancé in the wake of her death. But the longer she remains close, the more he falls apart. Rachel must make a choice—stay near the man she loves, or let go and move beyond.

Forever Thirteen (Book 2 of the Forever After series)

Joey Ashby died with his mother in a car accident when he was only thirteen. Being stuck forever at such an awkward age is bad enough. But when Joey sees the trauma his bullied best friend is facing in life, he knows he needs to step in. However, there's only so much a spirit in the afterlife can do.

Reclaim Your Creative Soul (non-fiction)

If you're a writer, artist, or musician with a full-time job or young family, you know how hard it is to find time for the creative side of your life. Through tips on organizing your creative space, budgeting your money, getting in touch with your spiritual side, and more, this book promises to help you find time for your craft—even if you can't quit your day job.

See all of Crissi Langwell's books at crissilangwell.com.

crissilangwell.com